An ode to crickets

I've never known a life without crickets before. Mrs. Brisbane says they are smelly. I think they smell fabulous!

Mrs. Brisbane says they can be lucky. I think I'm lucky every time I catch a cricket. And I thank them for that!

As I think about crickets so much that night, I burst into one of my favorite songs.

> Sing, all you crickets,
> For life's short but sweet.
> Sing, all you crickets,
> You're so good to eat!
>
> Sing, all you crickets,
> For your zesty flavor.
> Thank you, dear crickets,
> It's you that I savor.
>
> Sing, all you crickets,
> For being a treat.
> Thank you so much for
> Your life short but sweet.

Look for all of the adventures in Room 26

Don't miss
Betty G. Birney's chapter books for younger readers

Life according to
Og the Frog

according to

Betty G. Birney

PUFFIN BOOKS

PUFFIN BOOKS
An imprint of Penguin Random House LLC, New York

First published in the United States of America by G. P. Putnam's Sons, 2018
Published by Puffin Books, an imprint of Penguin Random House LLC, 2019

Visit us online at penguinrandomhouse.com

THE LIBRARY OF CONGRESS HAS CATALOGED THE G. P. PUTNAM'S SONS EDITION AS FOLLOWS:
Names: Birney, Betty G., author.
Title: Life according to Og the frog / Betty G. Birney.
Description: New York, NY: G. P. Putnam's Sons, [2018]
Summary: "Og the Frog tells the story of how he first came to Room 26, where he meets
Humphrey the hamster, befriends the students, and writes poems and songs"
—Provided by publisher.
Identifiers: LCCN 2017028971 (print) | LCCN 2017040532 (ebook) |
ISBN 9781524739959 (Ebook) | ISBN 9781524739942 (hardcover)
Subjects: | CYAC: Frogs—Fiction. | Pets—Fiction. | Schools—Fiction. | Hamsters—Fiction.
Classification: LCC PZ7.B5229 (ebook) | LCC PZ7.B5229 Lif 2018 (print) | DDC [Fic]—dc23
LC record available at https://lccn.loc.gov/2017028971

Puffin Books ISBN 9781524739966

Printed in the United States of America
Design by Eileen Savage
Text set in Warnock Pro

5 7 9 10 8 6 4

Thanks to the fabulous "Thirdies" (you know who you are),
who make my life better on so many levels!

CONTENTS

. . . .

My Leap into Room 26

. . . .

IT'S RIGHT THERE in the tall grass ahead of me. Just about the juiciest tidbit I've ever seen. Nice and chubby with spiky legs and wiggly antennae. A real dream of a cricket.

Now all I have to do is grab it with my great, long tongue and flick it back into my mouth and YUM! The time is right—

"SQUEAK-SQUEAK-SQUEAK!"

BOING! There's no cricket in sight. Not even any tall grass. I guess it was just a daydream.

Instead of the swamp, I'm in my tank in Room 26 of Longfellow School, and that furry guy in the cage next door is at it again.

"SQUEAK-SQUEAK-SQUEAK!" I haven't been here long, but so far, that's all he says in his high-pitched little squeal.

I've never seen anyone in the swamp like him.

He's hairy with beady little eyes and big whiskers. Kind of like a mouse with a short tail, but chubbier. His fur is an odd shade of yellowish brown—is that natural? And then there's the constant, high-pitched squeaking. (I think he's a little bit wacky.)

My skin feels dry, so I plop myself into the large bowl of water in my tank.

SPLASH!

The water here is a lot cleaner than it was back in the swamp where I used to live. The teacher puts in fresh water every day. It's nice, although a little bit of muck never hurt anybody.

"A little less splashing over there," the teacher says. I pop my head up above the water and see that she's smiling at me.

"Who . . . me?" I ask.

Some of the students giggle. They *like* to giggle.

I haven't been in school for long, but I have figured out that the big human is the teacher and the smaller humans are her students. It's just like Granny Greenleaf teaching the little tadpoles back in the swamp, but these tads are much bigger.

I have no idea why the furry guy and I are here. We don't have a single thing in common with the humans or each other.

Don't get me wrong. While the squeaking sometimes gets under my bright green skin (with snazzy black polka dots), I'm glad to be living in Room 26 and out of Room 27.

I'd rather be back in the swamp, but I was hoppy to go anywhere to get away from George.

In fact, for a while all I could think about was getting away from George.

George is the *other* frog back in Miss Loomis's class, where I started out at Longfellow School. He was *not* a nice frog. To be fair, until I came along, he was the only frog in Room 27. I guess he liked it that way.

But it wasn't my idea to move to a classroom. I was content to live in the swamp. It was a paradise for frogs, offering every kind of yummy insect you can imagine!

I ate crickets for breakfast, dragonflies for lunch, beetles and grasshoppers for dinner and mosquitoes as a bedtime snack. There were also lovely snails and other small crunchy creatures. Yum! There was plenty of water to keep my skin wet, and there were damp, grassy places where I could hide.

I had to do that often, because there was danger, too. Beaky birds and slithery snakes. Lurking lizards and some furry foes as well.

But I can swim, and I can leap, and it was always just a hop, skip and a jump to safety! Once I reached a soggy and sticky hideaway, I could daydream to my heart's content. And I do like to daydream!

Every morning, I looked up at the sky and sang a joyful song.

> Let us sing to life in the swamp,
> Where we hop and leap and romp.

What's that I see over there in the thicket?
Joy, oh joy, it's a lovely cricket!

As I sit in the morning dew,
Swamp, oh swamp, I sing to you!

I thought that George might like my song, but no, he most definitely did not. There was nothing he liked about me.

You see, George is a bullfrog, and it's well known that bullfrogs are the bullies of the swamp.

For one thing, they are BIG. They are also loud and bossy. You get a group of bullfrogs together at night, and you won't believe the racket! They call it singing. I call it an uproar.

The worst was a critter named Louie the Loudmouth. Louie was all mouth and no brain. I think he was related to George.

Louie mouthed off nonstop, until one day when a long-legged crane silenced him forever. There was peace in the swamp at last.

But there was no peace with George in Room 27.

He was a bully who took an instant dislike to me and let me know it.

George said *terrible* things to me, day in and day out. I won't repeat any of it, because he said insults that tadpoles—big or small—should never have to hear!

It was awful, but thankfully I learned to block it out, so I heard what the humans heard:

"RUM-RUM. RUM-RUM. **RUM-RUM. RUM-RUM!**"

Sometimes I'd politely answer with the clear, strong call of a green frog.

"BOING!" I'd say. "Oh, really? You think so?"

Ordinary frogs may croak, but green frogs like me have a special twanging sound.

"Who says?" I'd repeat with a boing.

Green frogs are proud of our twangs. When we go boing, every critter in the swamp knows exactly who we are.

But George wasn't impressed. He got even louder.

"RUM-RUM. RUM-RUM!"

And so it went, all day long. All that noise made Miss Loomis as jumpy as a jackrabbit. She could hardly teach because George was so loud.

The problem didn't stop at night, either. I'm not sure George ever slept, because he kept up a steady stream of RUM-RUMs all night long.

There was never time to do what I like best: Float. Doze. *Be*. That's when I just let my mind drift like a cloud. I always get my best ideas this way.

So when Miss Loomis explained to the class that I'd be

leaving Room 27 and moving to Room 26, my heart started beating like a hummingbird's wings.

I didn't know anything about Room 26, but it *had* to be better than living next door to George. Anyplace would be better without George.

The teacher in Room 26 is called Mrs. Brisbane, and she seems nice. She's not a bit jumpy, like Miss Loomis was. She's as steady as a salamander.

She speaks in a voice that's soft but not too soft. She has a nice smile and sharp eyes like an eagle that could quiet even George down with a single glance. (Well, maybe.)

In my short stay in Room 27, I learned to piece together some of the sounds humans in the classroom make. But it wasn't easy with George going **RUM-RUM** all the time.

A lesson in Room 27 sounded like this: "Class, take out your books and turn to page **RUM-RUM!**"

Or, "The capital of Spain is **RUM-RUM, RUM-RUM!**"

It's a wonder the students learned anything.

I found out more about human speech over the holidays, when Miss Loomis took George and me home for the break. Of course, she couldn't leave us near each other without George rattling off a thunderstorm of **RUM**s. So she put him in a room at one end of her house and put my tank in a room at the other end.

I was in the room with the picture box—which I later learned is called a television.

Sometimes Miss Loomis would fall asleep while watching, and the television would be on all night. That's when I really learned to understand human talk. Words like *news* and *pain relief*. And the quiz shows were very educational.

For instance, did you know that there are places called deserts that get less than ten inches of rainfall a year? I don't think my frog friends and I will be moving to a desert anytime soon!

And the capital of Spain is actually Madrid.

The most fascinating fact I learned from a game show is that the longest frog leap that has been recorded is—are you ready?—33 feet, 5.5 inches! I'm going to need a lot of practice to beat that record!

Of course, I don't have that much room to leap in my tank.

 ❧ ❧ ❧ ❧

When I first came to Room 26—with Mrs. Brisbane's nice voice and no George to interrupt—I was able to hear what was going on for a change.

Miss Loomis carried my tank into the classroom, and the students were as excited to see me as I am when I zero in on a cricket.

All eyes were on me as she explained about George not getting along with me. Including a pair of beady little eyes that belonged to the scrawny little fluff ball in the cage next to me.

Someone made a strange noise—"Ribbit." It didn't sound like anything I'd heard back in the swamp, but everyone laughed again.

When Mrs. Brisbane said that I'd make a nice friend for Humphrey, I heard a little squeak from the furry guy next door. He must be called Humphrey!

After Miss Loomis left, the students gathered around my tank for a closer look. All except one, a red-haired girl who looked as miserable as a toothless swamp beaver.

The students had a lot of questions, and Mrs. Brisbane had the answers. She explained that I am an amphibian, so I am cold-blooded.

She said that hamsters like Humphrey are warm-blooded. So Humphrey must be a hamster!

I heard some tiny squeaks coming from next door . . . and then I let out a great, big "BOING!"

The students burst into laughter. They all laughed every time I said, "BOING!"

It was like a game. I'd say, "BOING," and everybody would laugh.

A boing may mean I'm happy or sad or may be an answer to a question, but unfortunately, humans can't understand me.

When the big tads wanted to know what I eat, Mrs. Brisbane told them, "Miss Loomis said he likes insects," which is true. Just thinking about a nice, juicy cricket makes my tongue tingle.

But the students all said, "Ewwww!" and made faces. Except for Humphrey, who let out a series of three high-pitched squeaks.

"SQUEAK-SQUEAK-SQUEAK!"

I'm not sure you'd even hear him in the swamp, with all the loud animals there, especially the bullfrogs. Still, his squeaks don't sound mean like George's rumblings. He seems harmless but slightly irritating, like a furry fly. And he's such a fuzzy little thing, he's no threat to me. He couldn't even scare a slug.

Mrs. Brisbane assured them that eating crickets is normal for frogs—yes, ma'am! Luckily, Miss Loomis had sent a jar of crickets along with me. Life is better with a jar full of crickets—and no George.

From when I first got here this morning, I thought Room 26 would be an improvement over Room 27. But as Granny Greenleaf always said, "Only time will tell."

⚓ ⚓ ⚓

Just like in Miss Loomis's room, when a bell rings in Room 26, the big tads all leave the classroom, but the furry fellow and I stay.

BING-BANG-BOING! Without George, the quiet is a relief.

I am just about to doze off when I hear that sound again.

It's something squeaky, but this time it doesn't sound like the furry guy.

Screech-screech-screech!

I glance over at his cage, and what do you know? My tiny neighbor is running inside a great big wheel.

Screech-screech-screech!

Snakes alive! Who spins in a wheel? Nobody in the swamp does that.

Then he starts squeaking.

"Squeak-squeak-squeak!"

Screech-screech-screech!

It isn't nearly as bad as being around George, but suddenly, I am a little homesick for the buzzing, humming, rustling, rattling, croaking, chirping and swishing sounds of the swamp.

I climb into my water bowl to reflect on my day. It's easier to think when I'm damp.

The screeching and squeaking sounds are a lot softer underwater. But then the bell rings, which even underwater, I can hear.

The students come back, and soon Mrs. Brisbane is talking about my old home. Wow! I never knew how old the trees around the swamp might be! Even older than old Granny Greenleaf!

It's odd to spend all afternoon indoors. Back in the swamp, I spent my afternoons looking for food. (Sometimes I came up short.) Of course, I don't have to do that now.

I don't have anything to do here. It's an easy life (but maybe a little dull).

After a while, the bell rings one more time.

I pop my head up and watch as the students leave again: the boy with glasses who's always the first out the door, the loud boy, the shy girl, the giggling one.

Before long, the furry guy and I are all alone in Room 26.

I snooze on my rock for a while, but it's not easy to sleep with that round thing on the wall ticking so loudly.

The humans look at it to know what time it is. I guess they never thought of just looking up at the sky: the sun, the moon and the stars. You can tell what time it is in the swamp without ticking noises or loud bells.

The room slowly turns dark, and I am hoppy that the furry guy is quiet. Maybe he's dozing, too.

And then, all at once, my neighbor flings open the door of his cage and scurries over to my tank. Wouldn't you think somebody would put a lock on that door?

"SQUEAK-SQUEAK-SQUEAK! SQUEAK-SQUEAK-SQUEAK-SQUEAK!" he says in a very excited voice.

I think he's trying to tell me something. Does he think I understand?

Frogs and furry creatures are *never* friends in the swamp.

Still . . . he's a lot friendlier than George ever was.

I decide to give him a glorious green frog greeting.

I leap toward my neighbor and say, "Hoppy to meet you! BOING-BOING!" in my fabulous froggy way.

And would you believe it? The furry guy looks shocked.

He leaps backward, races to his cage and slams the door behind him.

After a while, there is only the ticking noise and the gentle song of crickets in the room.

So much for friendship!

My Learning Curve

· · · · · · · · · · · · · · · · ·

THE SUN DROPS in the orangey-pink sky, and the crickets begin their song. Every swamp critter joins in a farewell song to the sun. Soon, the owls and the bats will be on the prowl, so I hunker down in the tall, wet grass and wait.

Suddenly, Room 26 is as bright as daylight. I leap up just in time to see a tall man with what looks like a piece of moss above his lip pull something on wheels into the room.

Oh, boy—I must have been daydreaming, because this place isn't anything like the swamp. No owls, no bats, no grass, no sunset. Just a tank on a classroom table in Longfellow School.

But I know this man, because he also came into Room 27 every school night.

"Be of good cheer 'cause Aldo's here!" he says.

"Hello again!" I greet him out of habit. I think all he hears is "BOING!"

"Hey, I know you," he says. "The frog from down the hall. What are you doing here?"

Of course, the furry fellow chimes in. "SQUEAK-SQUEAK-SQUEAK!" And Aldo answers him. He even knows Humphrey's name. Does he speak Hamster?

I realize the name sounds like something the bullfrogs would say: RUM-**RUM**-**RUMPHREY**!

Aldo pushes a round red thing into Humphrey's cage. "Have a tomato, pal!" he says.

Humphrey gulps it in one bite, and his cheeks puff out. Whoa! I didn't expect that.

Aldo says he's sorry he didn't bring me something, then sits down to eat his dinner.

He talks while he eats, and Humphrey squeaks and squeaks some more. I can tell he likes Aldo.

And Aldo has big news—he just got married. The furry fellow squeaks back at him and does a triple somersault. He sure is excitable!

It's amazing to watch the man clean the room: sweeping, dusting and polishing. He's as graceful as a dragonfly and as busy as a bee.

Before long, Aldo is gone and the room is dark again.

I wait and listen. The furry guy is very quiet.

At last, it's peaceful in Room 26, until—

Scritch-scritch-scritch!

The scratching sounds are very loud.

I hop to the side of my tank that faces Humphrey's cage. What in the swamp is he doing?

I stare at him for a few seconds and then I get it. He's writing in a teeny-tiny notebook with a teeny-tiny pencil.

Scribble-scribble! Scritch-scritch-scritch!

This little ball of fur can write? Where did he get his notebook and pencil? How did he learn to do that?

For a hop, skip and a jump, I am a little jealous. Of course, my webbed toes wouldn't hold a pencil very well, and a notebook wouldn't last long in my tank.

Maybe he's just showing off. But at least he isn't as noisy as George. He doesn't call me bad names, as far as I can tell.

I decide to go for a nice soak in my bowl and let the water soften the scribbling sounds.

Ah! It works!

But I wonder what Humphrey is writing. Is he writing about me? If so, what does he think about me?

After a while, the soft swishing of the water washes all those thoughts away, and I can Float. Doze. *Be.*

I soak for a bit and then leap up to my rock. The ticking of the clock seems much louder than before.

In fact, it's almost as loud as nighttime in the swamp.

At dusk, the bullfrog chorus begins. Yep, I remember it well.

RUM-RUM!
We are the guardians, defenders of the swamp!
RUM-RUM-RUM-RUM!

We love to live in the weeds.
RUM-RUM!
We are the hero frogs, protectors of the swamp!
RUM-RUM! RUM-RUM!
We love to sing of our deeds.

If you ask me, it's not much of a song. Defenders of the swamp? If Chopper, the big old snapping turtle, so much as hisses at them, the bullfrogs hop away from their beloved weeds and disappear. I've seen it happen!

I run away, too, because none of us are a match for Chopper. But at least I don't pretend to be something I'm not.

The next morning, Mrs. Brisbane calls out her students' names. In turn, each one replies, "Here."

This is so helpful! I know all their names now.

A.J. is the one with the wide smile and very loud voice, but he's much nicer than a bullfrog.

And Sayeh is the girl who doesn't like to talk much. She's as sweet as honeysuckle.

Art has something in common with me. He likes to stare out the window and daydream. I wonder what he's thinking about?

Heidi is the girl who blurts out answers in class. She reminds me of Owlbert, who calls out questions all night long. "Whooo? Whooo?"

He hoots so much, after a while I think, "*Who* cares *who* it is?"

Seth can't sit still. He is as wiggly as any water snake.

And Mandy complains like the peeper frogs. They never let up. It's "PEEP-PEEP-PEEP" night and day.

Someone important stops in to greet me. I met him once before in Miss Loomis's classroom. His name is Mr. Morales, and he is the school principal. Apparently a principal is a very important human. He's wearing a tie with yummy-looking dragonflies on it.

I never saw a tie before I came to Longfellow School, but then I'd never seen a backpack or a chalkboard or a human up close!

"And how is your new pupil adjusting?" he asks Mrs. Brisbane.

"Very well," she says.

The principal peers down into my tank.

"Hi!" I boing at him.

He laughs. "I hear George has quieted down quite a bit since Og has moved," he says.

That must be a great relief to Miss Loomis!

As the morning goes on, I can understand the lessons, especially the one about frogs. Mrs. Brisbane puts up a chart with lots of pictures.

BING-BANG-BOING! I know those things! It shows eggs, tadpoles, froglets and a very handsome green frog who looks a lot like me.

The students listen quietly, and even Humphrey-Rumphrey doesn't squeak or screech his wheel while Mrs. Brisbane talks.

I can't believe my invisible ears. Mrs. Brisbane makes learning interesting—and there's no George to interrupt.

I just wish I understood Humphrey. All I get from him is "SQUEAK-SQUEAK-SQUEAK."

Most of the time, he's in constant motion, but sometimes he disappears into a funny little hut to sleep. At least I think he's sleeping, but who knows?

When he's awake, if he's not spinning his wheel or squeaking his head off, he climbs up the side of his cage. Then he leaps (though not quite like I do) to his tree branch and drops down to the bottom of his cage, which is covered with something soft.

If the bell rings, he hops on his screechy wheel. If a student asks a question, he goes "SQUEAK-SQUEAK-SQUEAK!"

If Mrs. Brisbane writes on the board, Humphrey climbs up to the top of his cage and hangs by one paw.

If I could talk with him, I'd tell him to take time to stop and smell the water lilies. Float. Doze. *Be.*

When Mrs. Brisbane talks about frog facts, her students are amazingly interested. I'm not sure that Humphrey is even paying attention until Heidi asks a question and he scrambles to the front of his cage to listen.

"Where did Og come from?" Heidi asks.

"From an egg," Mrs. Brisbane answers.

That sounds right, although I don't remember that part.

Heidi shakes her head. "No," she says. "I mean, how did he get to Miss Loomis's class?"

"Ah, I see," Mrs. Brisbane replies. "That's a good question. I'll ask her."

She goes on to talk about how I like to eat crickets. Mrs. Brisbane makes a face as she tosses one into my tank and I grab it with my tongue.

The big tads are very impressed!

I am hoping for another cricket when the girl called Mandy reaches in my tank and picks me up. Without even asking. It's a surprise, but not a pleasant one.

Then she loudly complains about me when I pee on her!

I don't *mean* to—it's just what we frogs do to protect ourselves when a stranger grabs us. And it works. Mandy drops me right away.

She complains about other things, too. Earlier in the day, I heard her complain about a girl named Tabitha. Mandy explained that she tried to get her to play, but Tabitha wasn't friendly.

"Maybe she's shy," Sayeh said. "I was shy when I came here at first, because I come from a different country and I was embarrassed that I didn't speak English very well."

"You were shy," Mandy agreed. "But you were always friendly."

Soon Mrs. Brisbane stops talking about frogs and starts talking about numbers and subtraction, but I don't understand a lot of what she says.

Here's what I know about numbers: I have one head. I have *no* tail (zero). I have four webbed toes on my two front feet and five webbed toes on my two back feet, which make me very strong and able to leap really high!

The most flies I ever ate in one sitting? Eleven!

And there are *hundreds* of singing bullfrogs back in the swamp. Way too many to count.

What else do I need to know?

While the teacher draws numbers on the board, I slide into the water bowl.

Time to Float. Doze. *Be.*

A little while later, Mrs. Brisbane catches my attention again when she reads something and talks about rhyming words.

Poems are new to me, but they turn out to be a lot like the songs I like to sing, without the music.

Rhyming words is easy peasy. Hey, that rhymes, too!

A few days later, the big tads groan when she tells them they have to write a poem, too.

They start to work, and there are more groans because some of them are writing about Humphrey—and they can't think of anything to rhyme with his name.

There's nothing that rhymes with *hamster*, either.

I am lucky that Og rhymes with *frog* and *log* and *bog* and all kinds of wonderful words! And I am starting to understand them all.

At the end of the day, I nod off . . . until I wake up to the awful sound.

Screech-screech-screech!

It's Rumphrey—I mean Humphrey—spinning that wheel. The students are gone, and we're alone again.

Suddenly, he leaps off his wheel and flings open the door to his cage.

Before I know it, he's pressed his hairy face right up to the side of my tank. Get a load of those wacky, wiggly whiskers!

"SQUEAK-SQUEAK-SQUEAK! SQUEAK-SQUEAK-SQUEAK!"

He looks right at me and squeaks his tiny lungs out.

I know he's trying to tell me something, but although I've picked up a bit of human talk, I still have no idea *what* he's saying.

Whatever I say, I know he won't understand me. And I don't want to jump and scare him again. So I just smile.

He keeps squeaking for a while, but we are getting nowhere. I am as frustrated as a nearsighted dragonfly trying to land on a twig on a windy day.

I guess Humphrey is frustrated, too. After a while, he gives up and goes back to his cage.

"Sorry, buddy," I mutter, but I don't think he hears me.

When Aldo comes in to clean, I am very grateful for the tidbit he tosses into my tank.

"Mrs. Brisbane asked me to give you this," he says. "Enjoy!"

BING-BANG-BOING! I'll say I enjoy it—because it's a *cricket*!

It tastes frogalicious, and I am very hoppy. (It isn't difficult to make me hoppy—really!)

"Thanks a lot!" I tell him.

He just laughs.

Later that night, I hear Humphrey scribbling in his notebook again.

Scritch-scritch-scritch!

Why do I feel as if he's writing about me?

After a while, he's quiet.

There's a nice light shining through the window—kind of like the moon perched on a post.

I feel content, and before long I'm asleep.

The Long, Long Weekend

· · · · · · · · · · · · · · · ·

Sunrise in the swamp. Is there a better time of day? The bats, owls and scary night creatures are in bed. The bullfrogs are still silent, and the dragonflies are just opening their wings. They are slowest before they limber up, so if I can only get into the perfect position, I'll have a lovely breakfast . . .

"Class? May I have your attention?"

That's Mrs. Brisbane's voice. I *was* paying attention to my plan to catch a tasty dragonfly, but back to reality.

I listen up, but all she says is something about lunch and the cafeteria, so I go back to daydreaming about that dragonfly.

When the tads come back from lunch, some of the students stop by our table.

"Hi, Og!" It's Art, the daydreaming boy. "You know what?" he asks. "Sometimes I forget to pay attention in class and stare out the window. Now that you're here, sometimes I watch you!"

"I watch you, too," I tell him.

He smiles and says I'm funny.

I notice Garth in front of Humphrey's cage, and he looks as happy as a fish with a wiggly worm in his mouth.

"Today is Friday," he tells the hamster. "My big day!"

Humphrey squeaks happily, so I guess it's a big day for him, too.

Soon, Tabitha stops by my tank. She looks as unhappy as a worm caught by a fish!

"Hi, Og," she says. "How do you like Room Twenty-six?"

Tabitha has hardly spoken to anyone in class, so I am surprised she is talking to me.

"It's not bad," I answer honestly.

When she hears my "BOING!" she breaks into a big smile. I think that must be the first time I've seen her smile.

"BOING-BOING!" I repeat, hopping up and down.

"You're so funny!" Tabitha says. "Don't you think so, Smiley?"

She looks to make sure no one is around, then reaches in her pocket and pulls out a small, worn toy bear with a big smile sewn on his face. "Smiley, meet Og."

It's not a real bear, thank goodness. (Real bears are even scarier than snapping turtles!) So I say, "Hi, Smiley!"

Tabitha giggles. "Did you hear that, Smiley? That's how Og talks. *BOING!*"

She giggles again, and that makes me hoppy. Mrs.

Brisbane calls the students back to their tables, but I feel proud that I made Tabitha smile.

I'm in a good mood . . . until the end of the day.

That's when Humphrey starts to squeak excitedly. Garth is excited, too.

Before long, Garth—with his pal A.J.'s help—throws a blanket over Humphrey's cage and carries him out of Room 26!

Mrs. Brisbane smiles as she watches them.

I am in shock! Are they kidnapping Humphrey? Or hamsternapping him?

If they are, Garth and A.J. sure look happy about it, and so does Mrs. Brisbane. It doesn't make sense.

I hear some weak squeaks from the cage as the boys leave Room 26. What is Humphrey trying to tell me? Maybe it's "good-bye forever!"

Poor little furry guy. Those boys seemed so nice . . . until now.

Then, Mrs. Brisbane leaves, too, and I'm all alone in Room 26.

When I was in Room 27 with George, I used to wish with all my heart that I could be alone.

But this is more alone than I've ever been.

What can I do? I am stuck in a tank with a lid on it. It's a nice tank with a large water bowl, a few plants and a dry place with rocks, but it's a lot smaller than the swamp.

There's nothing I can do to help Humphrey, the missing hamster. So I do the only thing I can think of: I take a nap.

I wake up when Aldo comes in to clean.

He doesn't seem concerned that the hamster is missing. He smiles and talks while he sweeps and dusts.

Watching Aldo is more entertaining than watching a hawk with a poor sense of direction.

I hold my breath hoping . . . and then he tosses me another cricket. I dine like the king of the swamp!

But once Aldo leaves, Room 26 is even quieter than on weeknights. I'm almost hoppy for the loud ticking of the clock, although I hardly notice it anymore.

So I do what I did on lonely nights in the swamp.

I sing.

Oh, give me a home
Where amphibians roam,
Where there's crayfish and turtles and fish,
Where seldom is heard
A discouraging word,
And the insects are simply delish!

Home, home in the swamp,
Where there's crayfish and turtles and fish,
Where seldom is heard
A discouraging word,
And the insects are simply delish!

I sing all the songs I can think of, and then it's quiet again, except for the clock.

With nothing better to do, I decide to spend a little time watching it, because it keeps changing. A small arrow moves in a slow circle, number by number, and a longer one moves around the circle faster.

After a while, I get it. The numbers stand for the hours. This might be very useful, especially in a classroom where I can't always count on watching the sun to tell what time of day it is.

The faster arrow must show the minutes. And there's a tiny arrow that races around the circle for the seconds.

Humans must be smarter than I thought!

The hour arrow moves completely around the clock several times as the weekend continues.

That's a long time, but at least I have clean water. And I'm used to not eating on a regular schedule like humans and hamsters do.

It would be easy to sit on a rock or float on the water all day, but I would get soft and flabby. After all, in the swamp I was constantly leaping and hopping and moving from dry land to water and back.

I decide to start an exercise program.

First, I hop into my water bowl and splash as hard and fast as I can. Then, instead of resting on my rock, I do jumping jacks (an exercise that is named for a friend of mine back in the swamp), push-ups and big leaps.

Each time, I leap a little higher than the time before.

When I look up at the clock, a lot of time has passed. I'm so tired, I fall right to sleep.

Before I know it, the door to Room 26 opens and Mrs. Brisbane walks in.

"Og!" she says, rushing to my tank. "You're okay! Miss Loomis told me it was fine for you to stay here alone, but I worried about you all weekend."

"I'm fine!" I tell her, hoping she'll understand.

"You certainly look well," she says.

I would think so! My skin is beautifully moist, and my muscles are in great shape for leaping.

Then the door opens again. Garth and A.J. are back with Humphrey's cage. I guess he wasn't kidnapped after all! Or, if he was, they got tired of his squeaking and brought him back.

Once Humphrey and his cage are back in place, he starts right in. "SQUEAK-SQUEAK-SQUEAK! SQUEAK-SQUEAK-SQUEAK!"

He seems happy to be back.

I decide to relax in the water, and after a while, the little fellow quiets down.

Everything seems back to normal, until the girl named Gail starts giggling. She keeps looking at my tank and laughing.

It turns out that someone has taped a funny note to my tank. I can't see it, but Gail can't stop giggling about it.

The *somebody* who put it there is Kirk, who likes to make people laugh.

He tells jokes a lot. Like this one: What kind of fly has a frog in its throat? A *hoarse* fly.

I chuckled so hard, I almost croaked!

Mrs. Brisbane takes the note off my tank, but I still can't see it. It has something to do with kissing a frog.

I wish I could tell the big tads that kissing is something we frogs *don't* do.

I haven't been in Room 26 for long, but I think that Kirk likes to call attention to himself.

In the swamp, that's not always a smart thing to do. For instance, there are some very colorful and showy moths and dragonflies who love to swoop gracefully over the water.

They're pretty, but I must say, the showiest insects don't last very long!

But the toads, who are dull and plain, blend in with the mud and muck and hardly get noticed!

Despite the interruption, our teacher gets class back on track quickly.

While I was hoping to learn more about the life cycle of frogs, Mrs. Brisbane starts the day with something brand-new that she calls a spelling test. The good news is I learn some new words. I like the sound of the word *jewel*.

She moves right from the test to the big tads' poems.

When the students read what they've written, I understand most of the words. Amazingly, *frog* is repeated a lot. So is *Og.* And *Og* is a part of *frog.*

The poems are all great, but maybe Gail's is my favorite.

> *Og is a green frog,*
> *And he's our classroom pet.*

I am? I've never thought of myself as a pet before. I've always been a very independent frog.

Being Gail, she stops to giggle before she reads on.

> *Of all the frogs I've ever seen,*
> *He's the Best One Yet!*

Wow, that makes *me* want to giggle.

Richie's poem is very clever, too.

> *Og the Frog*
> *Is not a dog.*
> *Or even a hog.*
> *He's an amphibian*
> *But not from the Caribbean.*

Richie stumbles over *amphibian* and *Caribbean,* and the teacher makes him repeat them. (That happens a lot with Richie.)

Then she calls on Tabitha to read her poem.

Tabitha looks scared. She pats her pocket where she keeps Smiley hidden.

Everybody's waiting to hear, but so far she hasn't opened her mouth.

"Go on! It will be fine!" I boing in encouragement.

Tabitha is startled, but she starts reading her poem. She goes so fast, it's hard to hear it all.

> *People-think-bears-are-mean-*
> *but-they've-never-seen-Smiley.*
> *He-doesn't-growl-or-make-you-sad-*
> *he-wouldn't-ever-be-bad-Smiley.*
> *I-don't-care-what-people-say-*
> *he-helps-me-get-through-the-day-Smiley.*

There's something sad about Tabitha and her poem. I don't understand it, though. And I don't understand why some of the other big tads roll their eyes when they hear what Tabitha says.

"What a *baby*," I hear someone whisper.

After everybody shares a poem, Humphrey's sad squeaks make me feel a little weird. Humphrey has been around longer than I have, but there aren't any poems about him!

Then Seth reminds him why. "We all still love you, too, Humphrey. But we can't think of any words that rhyme with *Humphrey* or *hamster*. Do you understand?" he asks.

Humphrey squeaks back.

I'm not sure what he's saying, but I can guess that he feels a little left out.

That's the way I felt back in the swamp when my best pal, Jumpin' Jack, played leapfrog with somebody else.

"Your name doesn't rhyme, but mine does!" I try to explain to Humphrey. I don't want him to be upset.

He squeaks back at me—but who knows *what* he's saying?

I certainly don't!

My Secret Past

. . . .

There's nothing like a splashing contest with my pal Jumpin' Jack. He splashes up a big wave, and I splash one even higher. Back and forth we go, until Granny Greenleaf tells us if we keep it up, there won't be any water left! But as we say in the swamp, "There's nothing better than getting muddy with a very special buddy!"

Oops! The bell for recess rings. I guess I was daydreaming again. Now I'm even rhyming in my dreams.

I notice that Sayeh doesn't hurry out of the room. Instead, she waits for Tabitha to get to the door. I'm surprised, because Sayeh is shy and doesn't like to talk. But she always tries her best and speaks from her heart. She's like my cousin Lucy Lou, who always croaked the truth.

"Way to go, Sayeh!" I encourage her. Maybe she'll have better luck at making friends than Mandy did.

I wish she understood the many meanings of *boing!*

Sayeh *does* talk to Tabitha, which makes me hoppy. Tabitha looks as if she needs a friend.

I am amazed to see that Tabitha is not friendly at all in return! She doesn't even smile or walk out of the classroom with Sayeh.

Why in the swamp would Tabitha ignore a nice girl like Sayeh? Is she stuck-up, like those bragging bullfrogs?

Before I hop into the water to cool off, I hear the screeching of Humphrey's wheel.

Screech-screech-screech!

The little guy seems upset.

Did he see what happened between Tabitha and Sayeh?

There's no use asking him, because all he'd say is "SQUEAK!"

I paddle around in the water for the rest of the afternoon. Being damp calms me down . . . a little.

Luckily, all that wheel running tires Humphrey out, and he disappears into his sleeping hut.

It's quiet now—the perfect time to relax. Float. Doze. *Be.*

While I am daydreaming, I think up a little poem.

> There is something I don't get
> About my fellow classroom pet.
> Humphrey is furry and he is small,
> But I can't understand his squeaks at all!

At least I manage to write a poem about Humphrey without trying to rhyme something with his name or the word *hamster*.

I'm a poet and I didn't know it!
I can make words rhyme—
at least some of the time!

After school, Mrs. Brisbane tidies up her desk. She reminds me of Granny Greenleaf. "Just because we live in the mud and the muck," she'd say, "that's no reason not to be tidy."

I am surprised when Miss Loomis comes into our classroom, carrying her coat.

"Thanks for giving me a ride," Miss Loomis says.

"Anytime," Mrs. Brisbane replies.

"I have that information you wanted about Og's past history," Miss Loomis says.

That news is very interesting to me. I hop up on my rock to hear what she tells my teacher.

"Want to stop for coffee to warm up on the way home?" Mrs. Brisbane asks. "You can tell me all about it."

Miss Loomis thanks her and says, "I'd love to."

That's all very nice for Mrs. Brisbane and Miss Loomis, but unless they take me along for coffee, I won't know what they're saying!

While Mrs. Brisbane puts on her coat, Miss Loomis comes over to my tank.

"How's your star pupil doing?" she asks.

Before Mrs. Brisbane can answer, Humphrey pops out of his sleeping hut and lets out a very loud "SQUEAK!"

The two teachers laugh. Soon the two of them are gone, and Humphrey and I are alone . . . again.

Naturally, my neighbor hops on his wheel. The endless stream of screeches is a little much for me.

So I try to think of something else: the swamp.

The end of the day in the swamp is busy and noisy.

There are no bells ringing like there are at school. But there's plenty of buzzing, chirping, flapping and even the occasional bloodcurdling howl. The chorus of bullfrogs is deafening, and of course, my green frog friends and I let out some hearty BOINGs so everyone will know we're around, too!

But once the humans have left Longfellow School and Humphrey jumps off his wheel, the room is as silent as a peeper frog who's lost her voice. It's almost too quiet.

I guess Humphrey agrees, because before long, he starts squeaking at me again. I think the little fellow is trying to tell me something, but all I hear is "SQUEAK-SQUEAK-SQUEAK-SQUEAK-SQUEAK-SQUEAK!" And on and on he goes.

"I don't understand a squeak you're saying," I tell him with a loud "BOING!"

He squeaks back, and I BOING back. We are having a conversation, except for one thing: *We can't understand each other!*

I give up trying to talk, and that upsets Humphrey more.

Luckily, Aldo arrives to clean the room. I have never been so hoppy to see anyone in my life! At least I can understand most of the things he says.

He says his nephew Richie is happy that Room 26 has two classroom pets now.

Oh, Aldo and Richie are related! And I guess Humphrey and I are both classroom pets. That's something we have in common.

He loses me when he talks about going back to school. Isn't he in school right now?

As he's talking to Humphrey and me, he pulls out a piece of paper that must have something to do with his plan.

Once he's gone, I worry that Humphrey will want to have another chat, but this time he doesn't even try.

🐾 🐾 🐾 🐾

Humphrey also gives me the silent treatment the next morning. But when the big tads come in, there is plenty of commotion in Room 26, especially since someone (Kirk again) has put a sign on Humphrey's cage that has Gail giggling and the other students laughing, too.

Humphrey scrambles up the side of his cage to try and see it and lets out a huge "SQUEAK!"

I'm not sure whether it's a happy squeak or not, and I can't see the sign from my tank.

"You think you're so funny," Mandy tells Kirk.

"Because I am," Kirk says.

"It's annoying," Mandy replies.

"Aw, Mandy, do you have to whine about everything?" Kirk asks.

He turns to the other big tads. "I'm funny—right?"

I guess he is, because everyone claps for Kirk except Mandy and Mrs. Brisbane, who gets class started.

I think Kirk is funny, but he doesn't always pick the right time for a joke.

Back in the swamp, I had a friend named Gilly who was a very funny frog. She had a way of puffing up her body so that it would almost double in size. When she exhaled, she'd let out a wild, high-pitched BOING that made us other frogs laugh, at least *most* of the time.

That's why we called her Silly Gilly.

But when Granny Greenleaf was giving us tads a lesson on cricket catching and Gilly did her trick, Granny got very upset with her.

"There's a time and a place for everything, Gilly," she said. "And when I'm teaching an important lesson is definitely *not* the time for silliness!"

The rest of us stopped giggling, and Gilly hung her head. Then, after lessons, Granny made Gilly repeat her trick over and over. She got so sick of it, she never repeated it again.

So today, I'm thinking Kirk needs to learn when it's a good time to be funny. And when it's not.

If only he could meet Granny Greenleaf!

Suddenly, I hear our teacher say, "I talked to Miss Loomis and got some information about Og."

Everybody looks at her, even Richie and Art, who aren't always paying attention.

I wonder if Humphrey is listening. I know *I* am.

"I asked Miss Loomis where Og came from," she says.

The big tads' ears perk up. Mine would too, if I had ears, but all I have are circles under the skin that vibrate when sound hits them.

"I found out that Og came from McKenzie's Marsh— that's a local pond," she says.

"*Swamp!*" I correct her. "McKenzie's Marsh is a swamp."

"Oooh!" some of the students say.

"Ahhh!" some other students say.

"The grandfather of one of Miss Loomis's students was fishing there one day, and he happened to see Og sunning himself on a rock," she explains.

I remember so well.

I'd just finished having a leaping contest with my pal Jumpin' Jack. I was tired from so much leaping, and Jack decided to look for a snack, so I was all alone on that nice sunny rock.

Suddenly, everything went black and I couldn't see a thing!

"Gotcha," a voice said, but I didn't know what that meant. I'd never even heard a human voice so close before.

I was bundled up and carried away. It wasn't too far, but

39

my skin was already starting to dry out. A frog's skin should *never* dry out.

Then suddenly I was uncovered, and I was sitting in a car. Of course, I'd never seen a car before.

The large man looked down at me and mumbled something I couldn't understand.

He was smiling, but I wasn't.

He rummaged around in a box, then took out a bowl and poured water into it. He put the bowl on the floor of the car and set me in the water.

Ah, relief! Thank goodness that grandfather knew frogs need damp skin.

When the car began to move, the water sloshed around the bowl. The man talked to me, but all I heard was "Blah, blah, blah."

I must admit, I was scared. Wouldn't Jack and the other green frogs wonder what happened to me? *I* wondered what was going to happen to me.

Everybody in the swamp knew about the *terrible thing* that happened to my cousin Gulper. He wasn't paying attention one day (as usual). So when he saw a tempting worm, he grabbed it without noticing that the worm was attached to a fishing line.

The last thing we saw was Gulper being reeled in and a human hand plopping him into a big bag.

Poor Gulper. He was careless . . . but he was family.

Hearing Mrs. Brisbane talk about my secret past makes me as rattled as a rattlesnake.

"The grandfather thought he was a good-looking frog," she continues. "And he thought his grandson might like him as a pet."

"No!" Miranda calls out. She's shaking like a cattail in a windstorm. "That's . . . kidnapping!"

It's actually frognapping, and I'm shaking just thinking about it.

"I don't know what to call it," Mrs. Brisbane says. "The boy's grandfather surprised him with Og. It was the student's idea to share him with the rest of the class," she continues. "Especially since they already had George. He thought they would be friends."

"Who was it? Which student?" Miranda asks.

"I believe it was Austin March," Mrs. Brisbane says.

Heidi jumps up and stands next to her table. "Austin rides my bus! Boy, am I going to tell him off!"

"That wouldn't be fair," Mrs. Brisbane says. "He's not to blame."

"Yeah, he's a nice guy," A.J. says.

"I'm sure his grandfather thought it was a good idea," Mrs. Brisbane adds.

"*Bad* idea!" I reply, wishing they could understand me, because it was *such* a bad idea. Why didn't they ask George first?

I know what he would have said. **"RUM-RUM!"**

"So that's how Og came to Longfellow School," she says. "And aren't we glad he did?"

"No!" Sayeh stands up next to her table and speaks loudly.

I am in shock. *She's* not glad I'm in Room 26? Maybe she's not as sweet as I thought.

I wonder what Humphrey's thinking . . . until I glance at his cage and see that he's disappeared into his sleeping hut again. Isn't he interested in my story?

"I agree with Heidi," Sayeh says. "Og should be in the swamp with his friends and family."

A.J. wrinkles his nose. "Maybe he doesn't belong here."

It is a blow, I have to say. I'm just starting to feel like I *do* belong in Room 26. Don't the big tads like having me in class?

Do they really want to get rid of me?

"Maybe he doesn't belong here, but he's here now," Mrs. Brisbane says. "We'll have to figure out whether he should stay."

Whoa! Mrs. Brisbane doesn't want me here, either?

I don't hear anybody say that Humphrey doesn't belong in Room 26.

I feel green with envy, the way I felt when Jumpin' Jack beat me in a leaping contest eight times in a row.

Eight.

Oh, but on the ninth try—BING-BANG-BOING! I left him in the dust—or at least in the mud.

Back in the swamp, even if the bullfrogs bragged and bullied, and even if there were snapping turtles and other unfriendly creatures, no one ever questioned whether I belonged there.

Now I am in over my head.

I don't know what to think, so I plop myself into my nice, clean water bowl to Float. Doze. *Be.*

This time, it doesn't work.

Thanks a lot, Austin March's grandfather.

At Home with the Brisbanes

· · · · · · · · · · · · · · · · ·

IT'S A FOGGY morning in the swamp. On most mornings, you can see everything clearly: the slithering snakes, the soaring birds, the insects darting and swooping. But in the fog, nothing is clear. All I can see are shadows ... but I don't know what they are. I hope the fog clears soon, because I'm getting hungry!

I come out of the fog when Mrs. Brisbane begins our lessons. I'm not sure I understand what she's talking about. Nouns, verbs. Adjectives? What kind of animals are those?

The thought of being chased by an adverb frightens me.

There are a lot of other things I don't understand.

Why does Tabitha seem so sad and lonely, and yet she acts rude when someone else is friendly?

And why on earth do the students always giggle at Humphrey's annoying antics?

I feel as useless as a toothless alligator.

In the swamp, I could hop to it and get things done. I'd grab a cricket with my tongue, challenge Jumpin' Jack to a hopping contest or discover a new puddle to soak in.

Here, I watch things happening, but I can't do anything to change them.

Late in the afternoon, Tabitha comes over to my tank. I hope she won't be rude to me!

"I think Heidi is being mean about you. I bet it's because you're new to Room Twenty-six." Tabitha sighs softly. "I'm new here, too. It's hard to get used to it. It's not like my old school."

"I know!" I tell her. "It's nothing like the swamp, either." My loud BOINGs make her smile.

"You probably don't even know what I'm saying," Tabitha tells me.

I do a couple of hops and say, "Yes, I do!" My BOING-BOING makes her giggle.

"You're funny, Og," she says. "Do it again."

"All right!" I hop again, because Tabitha has a nice smile.

"You understand me! But why do you always say 'boing'?" she asks.

If I tried to explain, she wouldn't understand. *I* would like to understand why she keeps Smiley in her pocket.

I don't think anybody in Room 26 understands Tabitha. At least not yet.

I don't think they really understand me, either.

"I have a new foster home and a new mom," Tabitha tells

me. "She's nice, and Mrs. Brisbane is nice, too, but I don't feel like I really belong here. Do you?"

"I thought I did," I answer. "But now I'm confused, too."

Tabitha grins. "I love talking to you," she says. "And when you answer back, it's almost like you understand what I'm saying."

I am trying hard to understand a lot of things. But I wish she knew that I realize how tough it is when so much has changed.

After Tabitha returns to her seat, Humphrey starts squeaking nonstop.

Is he jealous because she talked to me? Or does he understand her problem, too?

I know he didn't come from the swamp, but he might have had another home before Room 26.

No matter how hard I listen, one squeak still sounds exactly like another. I'm almost relieved when he stops squeaking and hops on that screeching wheel.

There's so much about Room 26 that is foggy to this green froggy!

And then it's Friday again, and Mrs. Brisbane says that Humphrey is going home with Miranda. I can tell Humphrey really likes her. He always scrambles to the front of his cage when she's nearby.

I can tell that she likes him, too. Whenever she looks at Humphrey, she smiles. She must enjoy squeaking more than I do.

But when Mrs. Brisbane announces the news, Humphrey's squeak sounds worried.

Luckily, before Miranda's dad comes to pick up Humphrey and his cage, Miranda tells him, "Don't worry, Humphrey. My dog won't be there to bother you."

My furry little neighbor perks up. "Squeak!" he says.

Now he's happy. I guess he doesn't care for dogs. For such a tiny creature, he sure is complicated!

At least I have a nice quiet weekend to look forward to, with no squeaking and no screechy wheels.

But I am surprised when Mrs. Brisbane comes up to my tank after school and says, "Og, I worried about you all last weekend, so I'm taking you home with me this time!"

If she's worried about me, she must like me at least a little bit. That makes me feel as cozy as a lizard snoozing in a sunbeam. I could almost jump for joy!

It seems strange to be riding in a car, especially with a blanket covering my tank. It reminds me of the bad day when I was frognapped from the swamp.

As I was carried away in the sack, I could still hear the muffled "BOING-BOING! BOING-BOING!" of my friends calling to me. "Come back!"

I hope they understand that I didn't have any choice.

There is a surprise waiting for me at Mrs. Brisbane's house.

His name is Bert Brisbane, and he is her husband.

Unlike most of the humans I've met, Mr. Brisbane doesn't walk around on two legs. Instead, he gets around in a chair with wheels. The way he rolls his chair in and out of doorways and around corners is very impressive!

I try to imagine myself in a chair on wheels, but it would be strange for a frog not to leap once in a while.

An even bigger surprise is that from the moment Mrs. Brisbane carries my tank into the house, Mr. Brisbane is very interested in me.

"A frog?" Mr. Brisbane leans in close to my tank. "Where on earth did you get a frog?"

"I told you, Bert. Angie Loomis couldn't keep him in her room anymore, and so I said I'd take him," Mrs. Brisbane tells her husband.

"I thought that was just temporary," he says.

I'm glad it's not, since I never want to be near that bullying bullfrog again!

"His name is Og," she tells him.

Mr. Brisbane smiles and nods. "Og the Frog. I like it. But what does my pal Humphrey think of him?"

His *pal*? My teacher's husband is a friend of the little guy next door?

"I'm not sure," his wife says. "I can't understand either one of them."

Then Mr. Brisbane turns toward my tank, looks me straight in the eye and lets out a loud "RIBBIT!"

I am so surprised, I hop back a few inches. Why do all humans think frogs say *ribbit*?

He does it again, in a very odd voice. "RIBBIT!"

"Bert, he doesn't understand you," Mrs. Brisbane tells him.

"Why not?" her husband asks. "He's a frog, isn't he? And frogs say 'RIBBIT.'"

"Not this frog," Mrs. Brisbane explains.

She's right. I never heard one of my fellow green frogs make such a silly sound. Not even a bullfrog.

Mr. Brisbane leans in closer. "Maybe he doesn't say anything at all," he suggests.

I can't stand it any longer, so I tell him, "I have a lot to say!"

Mr. Brisbane jerks back a few inches when he hears my boing. He looks as surprised as a flycatcher bird who's accidentally caught a bee!

"What on earth was *that*?" he asks. "It sounds like a broken guitar string."

"That's the sound this type of green frog makes," she says proudly. "The scientific name is *Rana clamitans*. I looked it up."

Mr. Brisbane just stares at me. "*Rana clamitans*," he repeats.

49

"But you can call me Og!" I tell him.

He bursts out laughing, and then do you know what? He lets out a very loud "BOING!" He even makes it sound twangy, the way I do.

"I think you two might speak the same language," Mrs. Brisbane says with a laugh.

I only wish we did!

As the evening goes on, Mr. Brisbane continues to watch me closely.

Thank goodness, Mrs. Brisbane insists that he come to the kitchen and eat dinner. Finally, I can relax.

But as soon as they finish, Mr. Brisbane rolls back to my tank and watches me.

What does he think this is, television?

I'm hoping the Brisbanes will watch television—especially a nature program, set outdoors. I wouldn't even mind seeing a show about hamsters, if it would help me figure out Humphrey.

Mr. Brisbane's *pal*, Humphrey.

All this attention makes me a little nervous, so I slide into the water dish and soak. I think it's boring to watch someone soak, but Mr. Brisbane seems to be fascinated.

He's full of questions for Mrs. Brisbane, who pulls up a chair next to him.

"Don't some frogs live in the water all the time?" he asks.

"There are all kinds of frogs—even frogs that live in trees," she answers.

That's news to me!

"If he had a bigger tank, he could swim around," Mr. Brisbane suggests.

I pop my head out of the water. "That's a great idea!" I tell him.

Mr. and Mrs. Brisbane both laugh at my loud boing-boing!

I'm still jumpy and jittery from all that staring, so I launch into my weekend workout to unwind: hearty splashing, followed by a set of jumping jacks.

I am surprised to see that the Brisbanes are impressed with my performance.

"Will you look at that?" Mrs. Brisbane says.

"That is one lively frog!" Mr. Brisbane replies.

After that comes my froggy version of a push-up.

Mrs. Brisbane gasps. "I didn't know frogs could do that!"

I finish off with a series of big leaps.

"I can hardly believe my eyes," Mrs. Brisbane says when I stop. "He's never behaved like that in class."

"I guess he wanted to put on a show for us," her husband replies.

I can hardly believe how exhausted I am! If I were warm-blooded, like humans, I'd have broken out into a sweat.

Amphibians like me don't sweat.

While I'm resting, the Brisbanes talk about frogs.

Mrs. Brisbane brings in several books, which they read together.

"Look!" Mr. Brisbane points to a page. "Some frogs can jump over twenty times their own body length!"

"I certainly think Og can," Mrs. Brisbane says.

I'm glad she thinks so. Me? I'm not so sure.

"That reminds me of an old joke," her husband says. "What do you get when you cross a frog and a bunny?"

I'm thinking the answer has something to do with hopping, so I'm surprised when he tells her, "A ribbit!"

I guess he already forgot that green frogs like me don't say "ribbit." Still, it's as good as any of Kirk's jokes.

Then he has another riddle. "What did the bus driver say to the toad?"

Mrs. Brisbane shakes her head, and Bert replies, "Hop on!"

If Mr. Brisbane had ever spent time with toads, he'd know I'm nothing like them. But I don't mind. He reminds me of one of my favorite swamp creatures, Uncle Chinwag. He's a kindly old green frog who tells good stories but also is a good listener.

I learned a lot from Uncle Chinwag, like how to make my boings carry a whole mile and how to catch a tiny mosquito with my big tongue.

He likes to tell jokes, too. I especially like this one: *What do they call an alien in the swamp? A* marshian!

I'll bet Mr. Brisbane would like that joke, but if I tried

to tell him, he'd just laugh at my "BOING-BOING! BOING-BOING!"

"This frog is a treasure," Mr. Brisbane tells his wife. "You should enter him in one of those frog jumping contests. They really have such things."

I like the way he thinks. Of course, I've been in many frog jumping contests in the swamp. Sometimes I even won!

Mrs. Brisbane sighs. "I like Og, but I do have a problem with him."

Those words would have given me a chill, but amphibians don't get chills. It's that cold-blooded thing again. But why on earth would she have a problem with *me*?

"Our classroom isn't anything like the swamp," she continues. "Is he happy in his tank? I mean, Humphrey has always lived in a cage—that's different."

That's the truth! That hamster is as different as any creature I've known, including crickets and mosquitoes.

"I didn't understand Humphrey at first," she says. "But he seemed so happy. He helped the students. And when I brought him home, he cheered you up."

Mr. Brisbane nods. "I was pretty hard to live with after the accident that landed me here." He pats his wheelchair. "But Humphrey did help."

Humphrey? Are they talking about the Humphrey I know? The annoying neighbor in the cage next door?

"He helps everyone," Mrs. Brisbane agrees. "He really goes beyond his job as a classroom pet."

Wait a second! Being a classroom pet is a *job*? I'd never thought of that before.

And if it is a real job, will I be the first classroom pet ever to be fired?

Mrs. Brisbane rises. "I'll make some tea."

Mr. Brisbane follows. "I'll get the cookies."

The Problem with Me

· · · · · · · · · · · · · · · · ·

"Listen, always listen," Granny Greenleaf tells us tads. "You can learn more from a falling leaf or a passing breeze than from all the loudmouth bullfrogs in the swamp. And remember: Bad things happen when you don't listen," Granny warns us.

"That hit the spot," Mr. Brisbane says.

The Brisbanes are back. I may not have ears the way humans do, but I listen carefully to what they are saying.

"Now tell me about your problem with Og," Mr. Brisbane says.

"The biggest problem is . . ." she begins.

I can't imagine what's coming next.

"The crickets!" she continues.

"Crickets! What's wrong with crickets?" I blurt out.

Bert chuckles. "I think Og has a problem with your problem with crickets," he says.

BING-BANG-*BOING*! Right again.

"Miss Loomis told me that according to her research, frogs like to eat live crickets," she explains.

Yum! I think.

"Oh," Bert says. "I think I see the problem."

The problem is, I can't get enough of them!

Mrs. Brisbane looks so upset, I feel sorry for her.

"I like crickets," she says. "They're thought to be lucky in some countries. And I know some people think their chirping is annoying, but I don't."

I like their chirping, too. It helps my fellow frogs and me zero in on their location.

Just thinking about yummy crickets puts a smile on my face . . . until I look at Mrs. Brisbane.

She is not smiling.

"The thought of feeding live crickets to Og is so upsetting," she says. "Even though I understand that's what he ate in the wild."

True. On a perfect day, I ate crickets. On other days, I made do with less tasty bugs.

"Also," she adds, "that cricket jar has an awful smell. You know how I feel about bad odors."

"Can't your students feed him?" Bert asks.

Mrs. Brisbane looks down. I think she is embarrassed. "I can't ask them to do something I don't want to do. What kind of role model would that make me? I've been having Aldo feed him after school."

Mr. Brisbane nods. "Sue, I don't want you to be upset every time you feed Og. Are crickets the only thing frogs eat?"

"No," I tell her. "You could feed me mosquitoes and dragonflies and spiders, fish, crayfish, shrimp, small snakes and snails."

"BOING!" Mr. Brisbane snaps back in a very froglike way.

"BOING!" I answer, and I'm truly sorry that's all he hears.

"Oh, Bert," Mrs. Brisbane moans. "Do I sound silly?"

"Never," her husband says.

I have to admit, Mrs. Brisbane is the least silly creature I've ever met.

"And there's another problem," Mrs. Brisbane continues, looking at my tank. "Some of my students are upset that Og was stolen from his home and probably misses it. Some of them think he should be returned to the swamp!"

"BOING!" I say.

"Is that a good idea?" Mr. Brisbane asks.

Mrs. Brisbane bites her lip. "I don't know. I have to figure that out."

I'm not sure, either. If I'm not going to get any more crickets, I'll *have* to move back to the swamp. But how?

"Sue, let me do some research," Mr. Brisbane says. "Maybe you don't have to feed Og crickets."

"BOING????" Which is my way of saying, "I can't believe you said that!"

Is that his idea of being helpful?

Then I dive down into my water dish.

Mrs. Brisbane chuckles. "He's very entertaining," she says. "But I think before taking on a second classroom pet, I should have learned more about frogs and their environment."

Mr. Brisbane pats her hand. "But you have a good heart, Sue."

It's true. My teacher has a good heart.

I have a good heart, too . . . I think.

For many hours that night, I think about whether I want to stay in Room 26 or go back to the swamp.

I'm not quite sure how my heart feels about either choice.

Late that night, long after the lights are out and the Brisbanes have gone to bed, I turn my thoughts to my favorite subject: crickets.

I've never known a life without crickets before. Mrs. Brisbane says they are smelly. I think they smell fabulous!

Mrs. Brisbane says they can be lucky. I think I'm lucky every time I catch a cricket. And I thank them for that!

As I think about crickets so much that night, I burst into one of my favorite songs.

Sing, all you crickets,
For life's short but sweet.
Sing, all you crickets,
You're so good to eat!

Sing, all you crickets,
For your zesty flavor.
Thank you, dear crickets,
It's you that I savor.

Sing, all you crickets,
For being a treat.
Thank you so much for
Your life short but sweet.

I repeat the song several times (at least). I guess I shouldn't be surprised when Mr. Brisbane enters the room again.

"A singing frog?" he says as he rolls his wheelchair up to my tank. "Og, you are a creature of many talents. Your voice sounds just like a banjo, which is a fine instrument."

"Thanks!" I jump for joy several times. At least one human appreciates me!

"The thing is, Sue is a little squeamish about crickets," he explains. "And of course, you're not."

"Not one bit!" I tell him. "I do my job, and they do theirs."

"She really wants you as a classroom pet," he continues.

Now, those are words I have wanted to hear, even if I'm not sure what my duties are.

"If we could just do something about the crickets . . ." he says.

In my experience, there isn't much you can do about crickets . . . except eat them.

But Mrs. Brisbane is so kind to Tabitha and Sayeh and even me! I don't want her to be upset.

"Maybe we can make some changes," he says with a yawn. "So neither of you will be unhappy." He chuckles. "Or *unhoppy*!"

This is a human who speaks my language. He sounds so much like Uncle Chinwag.

Soon, he rolls back to bed, and it's time for me to rest as well.

After he leaves, it's very quiet and peaceful. There is time to think. Float. Doze. *Be.*

There is also time to worry about the cricket problem.

The next morning, Mr. Brisbane tells his wife that he's going to a place called Pet-O-Rama. As he wheels himself out to the car, Mrs. Brisbane watches from the window.

Then she turns to me and says, "Fingers crossed that he finds an answer."

I don't have fingers, so my webbed toes must do.

When Bert returns, he carries a big bag.

"Well?" Mrs. Brisbane asks.

"Pet-O-Rama came through," he says. "Now let's see if Og can do his part."

Can I do my part? I was always hoppy to splash water on Granny Greenleaf when she started to dry out on a hot day. And didn't I always volunteer to help the tiny tads with their leaping practice?

"I always do my part!" I tell them.

Bert answers with a silly "BOING." He doesn't sound much like a frog after all.

Mrs. Brisbane moves my tank onto the table.

"Here are our choices," he says, reaching into the bag.

Mrs. Brisbane and I stare hard as he pulls out a bright green jar. I like the color!

"Mealworms," he announces.

Mrs. Brisbane gasps. "I'm not sure what they are, but they sound awful."

I don't agree. A nice, wet worm can be quite refreshing on a hot day. And filling!

"You could give him a regular wiggly worm," Mr. Brisbane says. "But I think you would prefer these dried ones, Sue. They're called Mighty Mealworms."

"*Dried* worms? Ewww!" I gag at the thought of eating them instead of wet and wiggly worms.

Lucky for me, they think I just said, "BOING!"

Bert takes out some dried-up thing and tosses it into my tank.

I'm thinking no way, until I see Mrs. Brisbane's face staring hard at me.

"Oh, please, Og—like it!" she whispers.

She did say "please," so I give it a try. It has a crispy crunch and a tart worm flavor.

"Not bad!" I exclaim.

Mrs. Brisbane looks thrilled. "I think he likes it!" she exclaims.

"Humphrey would like these, too," Mr. Brisbane says. "The man at the pet store said so."

Really? Humphrey and I might actually like the same thing?

Bert reaches in the bag again. "Now, here is something called Froggy Fish Sticks."

I like the sound of that!

He opens a yellow jar and throws a tiny twig into my tank.

Twigs aren't usually tasty, but I see Mrs. Brisbane anxiously watching me.

What have I got to lose?

I grab the twig with my very long tongue and am pleasantly surprised. It's sweeter than the Mighty Mealworms. Crunchier, too.

"BING-BANG-BOING!" I say. "Not bad at all!"

Mrs. Brisbane smiles at her husband. "I think he likes that one even better!"

I do. It wasn't the same as a nice juicy cricket, but she looks so happy, I leap up and pretend to jump for joy.

"One more thing." Bert reaches in the bag again. What other delights does he have in there?

"Og will miss his crickets, so once in a while, you could give him a treat with this." He pulls out something thin and hollow, like a straw.

"It's a wand that will catch a cricket in a jar and you—or one of your students—can fling the cricket into the tank without touching it," he explains.

A wand! A *magic* wand, if it can fling crickets my way.

Mrs. Brisbane looks serious, but she nods. "I could do that once in a while. But the *jar*!"

"If you bring the jar home, I'll take care of cleaning it," Bert says.

"You are my hero!" I shout as I bounce around my tank.

The Brisbanes laugh. I don't care if they think it's funny.

The cricket problem is solved. I hope now that Mrs. Brisbane and I can both be hoppy.

I guess Mr. Brisbane is, too. Because the last thing he takes out of the bag is a lovely piece of moss which he adds to my rock.

"Thank you!" I say because Granny Greenleaf taught me to be polite.

"You're welcome," he replies.

Later that evening, I think up a song about mealworms.

Mealworms are mighty
And they taste all righty,
Though not quite as yummy
As crickets in the tummy.

Fish sticks are dandy
And they come in handy,
Though without the appeal
Of a tasty cricket meal!

Conflict and Confusion

· · · · · · · · · · · · · · · ·

I'M FLOATING ON a log through the murky waters of the swamp. I hear the distant buzzing of bees and the gentle swaying of the cattails. The sunbeams warm my skin as I close my eyes and feel the water lapping up and down beneath me. Up and down. Up and . . .

I open one eye and see that I'm not in the swamp at all! I'm in Mrs. Brisbane's car, and my tank is rocking up and down, up and down. I'm on my way back to school. Back to being a classroom pet, whatever that means.

Once my tank is in place, some of the big tads arrive and come up to say hi.

"Did you have a fun weekend?" A.J. asks in that loud voice of his. "I spent mine at Grandma's house. We made cookies!"

I think cookies are a tasty treat to humans, kind of like crickets are to frogs.

There are no crickets chirping in the classroom today. It's a little too chilly for them.

"Brrr! It's cold outside, Og!" That's Tabitha, rubbing her arms as she speaks. "Inside, too! Too cold to stay on the playground! Well, bye!"

I'm glad Tabitha talks to me, but I wish she'd talk to the other students, too. As Granny told us, "You can't make a friend if you won't be a friend."

As she and the others head to their desks, Humphrey darts to the side of his cage near my tank and out comes a long stream of squeaks. "SQUEAK-SQUEAK-*SQUEAK*!" he says again and again.

"There's no use telling me something if I can't understand it, buddy," I tell him.

Do you think he stops squeaking? No, he does not.

I don't BOING again because it just seems to encourage him.

Besides, it *is* cold in Room 26, and when the temperature falls, cold-blooded creatures like me slow down.

The tank is near the window, and it's getting chillier by the minute, until I am about to doze off. And when it's cold outside, we frogs can sleep a long, long time. Maybe even months.

But I wake up quickly when I hear loud voices yelling.

Or maybe I'm still asleep and this is a dream. Because everything in Room 26 looks different.

Instead of my friends sitting at tables that are neatly lined up, everything's been moved around.

Usually, the big tads read books, or write on paper, or

listen to Mrs. Brisbane. Now they are gathered in small groups, fitting together puzzle pieces, playing games and making things with paper and glue.

But two students are shouting at each other. They are as loud as George and his bullfrog relatives.

Instead of saying, "RUM-RUM," one of them is screaming, "CHEATER!!!!"

That is Gail yelling.

The other student shouts, "AM NOT!" right back at her.

That is Gail's best friend, Heidi.

From what I hear, they might not be best friends anymore.

Of course, my furry neighbor has to get into the act.

"SQUEAK-SQUEAK-SQUEAK!"

One thing I learned back in the swamp is that when there's trouble, it's best to keep your mouth shut. Again, I quote Granny Greenleaf: "When you poke your nose into other folks' arguments, you just might get bit!"

Ouch!

Mrs. Brisbane quietly takes control. "Girls, please!"

But they don't listen. Heidi and Gail are screaming at each other, cawing like angry crows.

It's as bad as the famous Battle of the Bullfrogs! I'd almost forgotten what a terrible day that was.

The more the girls squawk, the more Humphrey squeaks. "SQUEAK-SQUEAK-SQUEAK-SQUEAK-*SQUEAK!*"

Mrs. Brisbane stands right between the girls and says,

"Calm down and be quiet!" She sounds a whole lot louder this time.

The girls stop screaming, which is a good thing, because Humphrey stops squeaking, too.

Then Gail, who is almost always giggling, starts to cry.

And Heidi, who is always cheery, begins to bawl.

To me, this is a bad thing. In fact, it's something frogs don't do at all.

In the swamp, if somebody's angry, they don't cry— they do something about it. They squawk and swoop, they strike or sting, they even do worse than that. But crying? Never!

When Mrs. Brisbane gets them to talk, it turns out the girls had been playing a game and Gail believes that Heidi was cheating.

Heidi is sure that she was *not*.

Mrs. Brisbane reminds them that they are friends and can work things out.

"I'm not going to be friends with a cheater." Gail wipes her eyes.

Heidi sniffs loudly. "I'm not going to be friends with a liar."

Mrs. Brisbane sends Heidi over to a chair near my tank and Humphrey's cage and sends Gail to sit at the teacher's desk to cool off.

The argument makes me as sad as a lizard who just lost

a tail. (Even though it will grow back, a lizard still doesn't *like* losing a tail.)

While I'm thinking about sad lizards, the recess bell rings.

"Everybody gather up the games and supplies and put them back on the shelves," Mrs. Brisbane tells the students. "Recess is over."

Ah—now I understand. The students stayed inside during recess because it's so cold outside.

Mrs. Brisbane takes Heidi and Gail into the hall to talk. Room 26 is a lot quieter without them! I decide to sit in the water. Time to Float. Doze. *Be.*

The cold gets to me again, and I do more dozing than I expected, and I am surprised when the bell rings for recess again.

"Can we go build a snowman?" A.J. asks.

I can tell some of the other students like that idea, but Mrs. Brisbane says there's not enough snow for a snowman, and it's too cold to go outside.

I climb onto my rock, look out the window and see feathery little flakes drifting down from the sky. I've never seen snow before. It looks like rain, but whiter.

For this recess, Mrs. Brisbane divides the class into teams to play a guessing game. They stand in four lines, and she asks questions one by one. If a big tad on one team gets the question wrong, that person has to sit down.

A.J. gets a question about giraffes right, but he misses one about flowers and has to sit down.

Sayeh seems to know everything . . . until she misses a question about basketball.

Tabitha answers it correctly, and she smiles when she hears me say, "BING-BANG-BOING! Keep it up!"

It doesn't take long to notice that Tabitha gets *all* the questions about sports right, and her team cheers her on.

"Go, Tabitha!" they shout excitedly.

She looks my way and gives me a thumbs-up. I'd like to give her one back, but it doesn't work with webbed feet.

Seth, who is the team captain, high-fives her, and she smiles again.

For at least a few minutes, everybody likes Tabitha, and I can tell she likes them back.

She's so good, even people on the other teams cheer her on.

In between my encouraging boings, I can hear Humphrey squeaking excitedly.

In the end, Tabitha's team scores way more points than any other team, and everybody cheers for her.

It's nice to see her look happy for a change.

But when I glance at Gail and Heidi, they still don't look happy.

They look as if they've each just lost their best friend.

Once the big tads leave for the day, Room 26 is peaceful, until my nervous neighbor flings open his cage door and scurries over to my tank, squeaking like crazy and twitching his tail.

He leans in so close, he wiggles his whiskers right in my face! Thank goodness there's glass between us or he'd tickle me silly.

"You know I can't understand you, don't you, Humphrey?" I boing extra loud.

"Squeak-squeak-*squeak*!" he repeats again and again.

I hop a few times to seem friendly, and he finally leaves.

My mind drifts back to the swamp. I had a lot of good friends there, especially my green froggy friends. There were some bad guys, too. But at least I *understood* all of them.

I'm still thinking of my old home when Aldo comes to clean.

When he takes a break to eat, he pulls a chair up to Humphrey's cage, which is fine with me. Humphrey squeaks on and on.

Even though I'm not really listening, I hear Aldo talk about his dream of going back to school and becoming a teacher.

I don't think I'd like to be a teacher if I had to deal with irritating classroom pets like Humphrey and George.

A nice green frog like me would be okay, though.

He waves a piece of paper in front of Humphrey's cage. It doesn't look important to me, but it has something to do with becoming a teacher. It sure seems important to Aldo.

When he leaves for the night, I spot the paper half hidden under Humphrey's cage.

Aldo will be upset when he finds out it's missing.

For once, Humphrey and I agree on something, I guess, because later that night, Humphrey flings open his cage door.

I'm hoping he won't come squeak at me, and he doesn't.

Instead, he carefully pulls the paper out in the open and then—well, it can't be, but I think he's reading it!

It's a big piece of paper, so he has to skitter along each line and then scramble down to the next line to read every word.

It looks a little bit strange, but I give the little guy credit for working so hard to read it.

Maybe I should pay more attention to Mrs. Brisbane's teaching!

I shouldn't be surprised by anything odd that Humphrey does anymore, but I am caught off guard when he carefully drags the paper near my tank and squeaks at me.

"What am I supposed to do?" I ask. "I can't even see it from here. And if you drop it in the tank, the water will ruin it."

Humphrey gives me a long, sad stare and returns to his cage.

But he leaves the paper right out in the open. I'm hoping that Mrs. Brisbane will see it in the morning.

I'm extra careful not to splash it.

Maybe that's the kind of helpful thing a classroom pet does.

Stay, Go, I Don't Know

· · · · · · · · · · · · · · · · ·

IT'S CHILLY IN *the swamp—as cold as a snapping turtle's*
heart. Where's the bright yellow dot in the sky? Where are the
nice, juicy insects? And why can't I open my eyes?

There is no yellow dot in Room 26 in the morning—just
the cold white glow from the bulbs hanging above us. There
are no snapping turtles, either, but it *is* chilly.

"And how is my very, very favorite hamster? Oh, you're
looking so fluffy and warm!" a friendly voice says.

Fluffy?

It turns out that Mrs. Brisbane has arrived, and she's
talking to Humphrey. I hardly recognize her because she's
bundled up in so many clothes, she looks fluffy and warm,
too. No wonder she likes Humphrey so much. Although I
don't see what's great about being furry.

I think my shiny green skin is a lot nicer.

Then our teacher turns to me.

"Good morning, Og!" Mrs. Brisbane peers into my tank.

"It's very cold outside, so we'll make sure you stay warm today."

"Great!" I reply. When she turns her sunny smile on me, I really do feel warm all over.

Maybe this will be a fine day in Room 26 after all.

The students hurry into the classroom. Some of them rush up to my tank.

"Hi, Oggy-woggy-froggy!" Kirk greets me.

"Did you have a nice evening, Og?" Sayeh whispers in her soft voice. "Did you miss us?"

"YES!" I shout.

She and the other students gathered around all laugh because what they hear is a big, fat "BOING!" They like it, so in a hop, skip and a jump, I boing again.

Mrs. Brisbane laughs and then she heads to her desk.

At this point, Humphrey goes berserk. "SQUEAK-SQUEAK-SQUEAK-SQUEAK-SQUEAK!" he shrieks again and again.

Is he jealous because I am getting a little more attention than he is?

I don't think so, because he's very focused on something outside of his cage.

I hop up and down so I can get a better look. And then I understand.

He's trying to tell Mrs. Brisbane about the piece of paper Aldo left behind.

I want her to pick it up, too, because I like Aldo.

So I hop up and down some more, like a mad muskrat who just stepped into a hive of bumblebees. "BOING-BOING! BOING-BOING!" Translated, that means, "PICK IT UP!"

Mrs. Brisbane turns toward us again. "What is the matter?" she asks, walking back over.

Humphrey and I keep it up. "SQUEAK!" "BOING!" "SQUEAK!" "BOING!"

"What's this?" Mrs. Brisbane asks.

And then—whew!—she picks it up. That's good.

But instead of reading it, she folds it up and takes it back to her desk.

Humphrey and I squeak and boing and hop and holler.

"What's wrong with them?" A.J. asks.

"I don't know," Mrs. Brisbane says. "But Humphrey and Og seem very interested in this paper."

She opens it up again and reads it—but silently. She mumbles something about giving Aldo a call.

"Tell us what it says!" I call out.

"SQUEAK-SQUEAK-SQUEAK!" Humphrey says.

Unfortunately, Mrs. Brisbane tucks the paper in her desk drawer and starts class.

Humphrey staggers into his sleeping hut. I guess all that excitement wore the little fellow out.

The teacher is not even finished taking attendance when

Heidi starts waving her hand. That's good, since she usually forgets!

Mrs. Brisbane ignores her as long as she can, but she finally calls on her.

"What *is* it, Heidi?" she asks.

"Mrs. Brisbane, I'm still really upset about Og," she says. "In fact, I'm boiling mad!"

"Simmer down," the teacher says. "Tell me calmly why you're upset."

"Yes, tell me, too!" I shout.

Some of the students giggle at my boings.

"Og was kidnapped from his original home. That's against the law! I told Austin that!" Heidi stands up and continues. "Og probably misses his family and friends! They probably miss him."

I sometimes wonder if my old friends miss me at all. By now, Jumpin' Jack might have a new friend to race. Granny Greenleaf probably has a whole new class of tads to teach.

For all I know, my friends and family are leaping and singing, just the way they always did.

I don't want them to be sad . . . but it would be nice if they thought about me now and then.

"We should return him," she continues. "We should call the police!"

Whoa! I'm not sure I want her to call the police. I'd rather be in Room 26 than in jail!

"But he's *our* classroom pet," Richie says. This time *he* also forgets to raise his hand. "He belongs to us."

There are sounds of agreement from my other classmates.

Is that true? I never thought of myself as being owned by anyone.

"Richie is right," Gail says. "Og is *our* classroom pet. We'd miss him so much if he went back to the swamp. I know he'd miss us, too!"

I think she has tears in her eyes.

Her former best friend, Heidi, disagrees. "But he was stolen from his home!"

I guess those two haven't made up yet.

When Mrs. Brisbane looks away and calls on Tabitha, Heidi and Gail stick their tongues out at each other.

They're not even trying to be friendly.

"It's hard to be pulled away from your family and friends," Tabitha says without looking up. "It's happened to me."

She swallows hard and pats her pocket. I'm pretty sure Smiley is in there.

"It happened to me, too!" I tell her. "BOING-BOING!"

When she hears my voice, Tabitha looks up from her desk for the first time.

I do miss my swamp buddies. I *don't* miss the ornery snapping turtles and obnoxious bullfrogs. And there's so much happening in the classroom, I haven't had time to think about the swamp as much as I used to.

Mrs. Brisbane stops and stares at the class. "What do the rest of you think?" she asks.

I can't believe that this whole room full of humans is arguing about *me*. It's nice that they're interested, but I'm not sure if I'll end up back in the swamp (possibly as a nice tasty dessert for Chopper) or in a jail cell.

Who knows—they might put me back with George. *That* would be *worse* than jail.

Up until now, I liked the attention . . . but now I wish the tads would forget all about me for a while!

Mrs. Brisbane calls on Garth. He doesn't say anything at first. He just pushes his glasses up the bridge of his nose.

"Maybe," he says, "maybe all animals should be in their own homes. I mean, maybe Humphrey should go back to where he came from, too."

Everyone turns to stare at him.

"No!" golden-haired Miranda says. I've never seen her talk out of turn before. "I have a pet dog, and I wouldn't want him to go back where he came from," she explains. "He came from the shelter, and it wasn't very nice!"

"Hey, I'd miss Og and Humphrey, too," Garth agrees. "But they were taken away from their homes."

Art isn't always paying attention to what's going on, but he suddenly moans, "Don't take Og away!"

A.J. agrees. "Right! He likes being here—right, Oggy?"

I'm thinking of the answer when Garth speaks again.

"It's not about what *we* like. It's about what's best for the animal."

Mrs. Brisbane takes charge again. "I don't think that Humphrey lived anywhere else except Pet-O-Rama."

Jumping jackrabbits! That's the place where Mr. Brisbane got the mealworms and other tasty treats.

"And I don't think they'd take Humphrey back after all this time," our teacher says. "Listen, let's put this aside for right now. We need to learn a lot more about hamsters and frogs before any decisions are made. We need to do research."

Anything to calm the big tads down, I think. Mrs. Brisbane sends my classmates down to a place called the library to find out more about Humphrey and me.

That's a good thing, because I need to take a nap.

I can't figure out this problem unless I have time to think. That's what Uncle Chinwag taught me.

Work a bit,
Play a bit.
Laugh a bit,
Learn a lot!
Float. Doze. Be.
And you will live so happily.

Granny Greenleaf and Uncle Chinwag taught me a lot, but they didn't teach me how to be a classroom pet. We don't even have classrooms in the swamp. All of our learning is done outdoors, under the blue skies and the tall trees and in the muck and mire.

How did Humphrey figure his job out? Or is he just naturally helpful?

When the class returns from the library, they all carry armloads of books. Mrs. Brisbane gives them time to read and take notes.

It's quiet again, and my mind drifts until Mandy waves her hand.

"What is it, Mandy?" Mrs. Brisbane asks.

"You've got to do something about *him*," she says, pointing toward the big tad sitting behind her, who is Seth.

"What'd I do *now*?" Seth asks.

"You keep thumping the back of my chair," Mandy complains. "You do it all the time!"

"I don't mean to, but I have long legs. Why don't you move your chair up closer to your table?" Seth asks.

"Because . . ." Mandy hesitates. "Because you should move *your* table back."

Seth looks behind him. "There's no room."

Mrs. Brisbane looks as irritated as a toad who is stuck in the mud.

"He's right. Mandy, move your chair up closer," she says. "You've got lots of room."

The girl scowls, but scoots her chair up.

When it's time for recess, Mrs. Brisbane asks Mandy to stay and chat.

"I'm sorry that so many things make you unhappy," Mrs. Brisbane tells her. "But I don't think Seth was doing it on purpose."

"He annoyed me," Mandy complains. "I couldn't concentrate."

Mrs. Brisbane nods. "But you are easily annoyed. I have an experiment I'd like you to try. The next time you're bothered about something, I want you to think quickly of something that makes you happy. Can you think of something that makes you happy?"

Mandy stops and thinks. She thinks for a while.

"You can do it!" I tell her.

And surprise! She breaks out into a smile and glances over at my tank.

"Og is funny," she says. "And so is that sound he makes."

Mrs. Brisbane nods. "Look at him—he always seems to have a big smile on his face."

Actually, that's just my big wide mouth. But I try to make it look extra smiley, to help Mrs. Brisbane.

"BOING-BOING!" I say.

Mandy giggles again.

"So the next time you're going to complain about something, why don't you look over at Og? He'll smile at you and maybe even make his funny sound," Mrs. Brisbane suggests. "And you might forget to complain. Will you try?"

Mandy looks down and nods.

I think she needs some encouragement. "BOING-BOING! BOING-BOING!" I tell her.

She looks my way, and I let her see my big, smiley mouth. I even hop up and down a few times.

Mandy laughs. "He's so cute!"

Me, cute? George and the bullying bullfrogs would give me a hard time about that.

But Humphrey gives an encouraging "SQUEAK!" I didn't even see him come out of his sleeping house.

"Look—Og and Humphrey are friends." Mandy is still smiling.

We are?

Humphrey squeaks some more.

"Remember, when you want to complain, think about Og," Mrs. Brisbane tells Mandy, and she sends her outside to play.

BING-BANG-*BOING*! I did something helpful!

"SQUEAK-SQUEAK-*SQUEAK*!" Humphrey tells me.

I don't know what that means, but it makes me feel good.

I hoppily decide to nap for a while, but I am pleasantly awakened by the frogalicious sound of a cricket chirping!

Has Mrs. Brisbane had a change of heart? Is she going to wave her magic wand and serve me up a gourmet meal?

"Chirrup! Chirrup!" Those chirps are beautiful music to a frog's ears.

There's a sudden commotion in the classroom as the students chatter about a cricket and some of the tads even leap out of their seats.

I guess Mrs. Brisbane isn't the only human who isn't as fond of crickets as I am. Or insects in general.

Somehow, Kirk is involved. I guess that's not a surprise.

Mrs. Brisbane tells him to find the cricket.

He scoops something up and throws it on Heidi—or at least he pretends to. Because it turns out the cricket sound is really coming from Kirk . . . and I have to admit, it *almost* sounds like the real deal.

I'm disappointed, of course. It will be mealworms again for me instead of a yummy cricket snack.

Humphrey Goes Haywire

. . . .

AH, THE PEACE and quiet of the swamp on a lazy afternoon. My belly is full, my skin is moist, and life is good. The bees are buzzing, the birds are singing, and a turtle floats by, saying, "SQUEAK-SQUEAK-SQUEAK!" Wait a second— hold everything. Turtles don't squeak . . . do they?

I snap out of my daydream and realize that the squeaking is coming from a furry little creature. Hopefully, Humphrey will stop soon, but even if he doesn't, I'll give him a pass. He's a much better neighbor than a bullfrog.

Then the bell rings and the class rushes out for the day.

As soon as the classroom is clear, Aldo shows up—hours earlier than usual.

This time, he didn't come to clean Room 26. He is here to talk to Mrs. Brisbane. It turns out that paper he left behind could help him get into a school where he'll learn to be a teacher.

The little guy quiets down long enough for me to hear

Aldo tell her that he's not sure he can be as good a teacher as she is.

I wish I could tell him *no one* could be as good a teacher as she is.

She says something about coming in to teach our class, and Aldo says yes.

Thank goodness he listens to Mrs. Brisbane. Like I said, everybody should!

I can't hear the end of their conversation because Humphrey lets out a stream of enthusiastic squeaks.

Luckily, he's quiet once the humans leave the room.

That gives me time to think about how hamsters are so much more complicated than frogs. To a frog, life is simple: Try to find food and try not to get eaten. Take time to smell the water lilies. Sit on a rock and think. Float. Doze. *Be.*

I don't think Humphrey will ever just *be.*

The next morning, Mrs. Brisbane calls on the big tads to give their reports on a very interesting topic: the differences and similarities between hamsters and frogs.

My guess? There are zero similarities and a million differences. I'm not wrong, either.

Garth's report explains that Humphrey is a mammal. Humans are, too. Mammals give birth to their babies.

Then Mandy explains that amphibians like me are hatched from eggs.

I don't appreciate the alarmed "SQUEAK!" from Humphrey.

An egg can be a very cozy place.

Art goes into more detail about warm-blooded animals like hamsters, and Sayeh reports about cold-blooded animals like me.

Humphrey has another squeaky outburst when she says the word *hibernation.*

Maybe Humphrey doesn't like to hibernate, but I think it's as nice and cozy as being in an egg.

Then A.J. explains that hamsters have cheek pouches where they store uneaten food. I must admit my reaction is "EWWW!" which comes out as a very loud "BOING!"

Finally, Miranda says that hamsters come from warm, dry areas. In fact, getting wet is bad for them.

So what's good for hamsters is bad for frogs. And what's good for frogs is bad for hamsters. No wonder we don't understand each other!

And yet, we're both classroom pets. He's just better at the job than I am.

Maybe that's because he has a lot more experience.

Later, as I sit on my rock trying just to *Be,* I notice something very odd. Seth hasn't gone to lunch with the rest of the class. Instead, he's talking to Tabitha about sports.

"Go, Tabitha!" I tell her, and when she hears my BOING, she smiles. Seth smiles back.

Maybe Tabitha is starting to enjoy her new classroom at least a little bit.

Seth goes on to lunch, but Tabitha stays to talk to Mrs. Brisbane.

It's quiet in Room 26 without the other big tads, and I can hear everything they say. Mrs. Brisbane encourages Tabitha to be friendlier.

"I want to, but it's hard," Tabitha tells her.

Mrs. Brisbane smiles. "I know, but some of the students have tried to reach out to you. Can't you try, too?"

"Yes, TRY!" I say, and Tabitha smiles and nods.

Then Mrs. Brisbane sings a little song.

> *Make new friends, but keep the old,*
> *One is silver, and the other's gold.*

I LOVE to sing, but I didn't know that Mrs. Brisbane likes to sing, too. Her voice is as cheery as a swamp sparrow greeting the dawn.

I repeat her song so I'll remember it.

BOING-BOING-BOING,
BOING BOING BOING BO-ING!
BOING BOING BOING-BOING
BOING BOING BOING BOING BOING!

Mrs. Brisbane looks over at me and says, "I think Og likes the song, too."

Maybe she's starting to understand me!

Then she tells Tabitha that she can take Humphrey home for the weekend (as if his squeaking and screeching is a treat). Tabitha looks as happy as a toad in a mud puddle.

I'm hoppy that she is happy.

In fact, I sigh a great sigh of relief. Maybe now I can stop and smell the lily pads. Or at least try to remember what lily pads smell like.

I'm hoping the rest of the week will be easy peasy, but there are a lot of bad moods when the big tads don't do well on an important math test. Mrs. Brisbane isn't pleased, and neither are her students. But our teacher is not ready to give up.

She gives each of the big tads a study guide and says, "We will try again. We will be having a math test on Tuesday, so please spend some time reviewing what we've learned."

Mandy's hand goes up. "Do we *have* to have another test?" she moans. "Because—"

"Mandy?" Mrs. Brisbane gives her a look. Even *I* know what that look means.

Mandy quickly glances over at my tank. I grin at her until my mouth aches and hop up and down.

She smiles. "Never mind," she tells Mrs. Brisbane.

I'm hoppy to be of service to our teacher!

"Put the study guides in your backpacks so you won't forget them," she tells the big tads as the bell rings.

Recess is usually calm and quiet *if* my furry neighbor doesn't squeak too much, but this day, it's anything but calm. Just when I think nothing Humphrey can do will surprise me, I'm amazed.

When the room is empty, Humphrey flings open his cage door, grabs hold of the table leg and slides down to the floor!

"Settle down, Humphrey," I try to tell him. "Be careful!"

But Humphrey has some kind of plan, I guess, because he skitters across the floor as fast as a water strider bug being chased by a beaky bird.

I can hardly believe my great big eyes as Humphrey races straight to Seth's backpack, which is on the floor next to his table.

What in the swamp is he doing?

I think his small brain must have gone haywire.

I watch as he uses his tiny sharp teeth to pull out the study guide Mrs. Brisbane just handed out. Why doesn't he want Seth to study?

Next, he drags the study guide all the way over to Tabitha's chair. He stops to look up at her backpack. If he's thinking of climbing up there, he'll have to learn how to fly.

"Be careful, little guy!" I shout.

The next thing I know, Humphrey takes his two front paws and grabs onto a cord hanging down from the zipper on Tabitha's backpack and tries to pull himself up.

"Tabitha already has a study guide!" I tell him.

I glance at the clock and am shocked to see that minute arrow moving extremely fast!

"Hurry back!" I try to warn him, although I have no idea how he's going to slide UP the table leg. It's a long way from the floor to the table, and I don't think I could do it even with my powerful leaps.

But it's too late! The bell signaling the end of recess blares. Alarmed, Humphrey drops the study guide and races back to the table.

"Hurry!" I tell him.

And then the most incredible thing happens! Humphrey jumps and grabs the long cord hanging from the blinds and swings back and forth, higher and higher each time.

I hate to admit it, but Humphrey is one strong and fast hamster!

But . . . can he catch a fly with his tongue? I don't think so!

My heart is pounding as the cord swings up to the top of the table.

"Careful!" I warn him.

And even though I can't believe my own eyes, when the cord is as high as the table, Humphrey lets go, flies onto the tabletop, and slides past my tank and straight to his cage.

He pulls the cage door closed just as Mrs. Brisbane enters the room.

I see him panting as he crawls under his bedding. He looks so small and so tired.

"Way to go!" I tell him. I really hope he understands me!

Mrs. Brisbane looks around the room. "Why is the cord swinging like that?" she asks aloud.

"SQUEAK!" I don't understand exactly what Humphrey's saying, but he sounds worried. Of course he is! If Mrs. Brisbane finds out why the cord is swinging, they'll probably lock him up and throw away the key!

I'm not sure what he was trying to do with the study guide, but I know he had a reason.

Mrs. Brisbane heads toward the cord and I decide to help the little fellow out.

"Look at me! Yoo-hoo, over here!" I shout in my best boings. Then I hop into my water dish and splash as hard as I can. All that weekend exercise has paid off!

Mrs. Brisbane turns toward me and tells me to calm down. Luckily, right then the rest of the students stream into the classroom, making enough commotion to distract Mrs. Brisbane from our table . . . and, most important, from the cord, which has now stopped swinging.

Once the big tads are settled in their chairs, I hear a tiny squeak. It's Humphrey.

Is he saying thank you? Or am I just imagining things?

"You're welcome," I answer. Maybe this time he even understands me.

The poor little guy looks frazzled. I'm a little frazzled myself, so I plop into my water and try to *Be*.

It's not easy to *Be* when you have a hamster for a neighbor.

I can't help noticing that just before the bell rings to signal the end of the day, Mrs. Brisbane spots the study guide on the floor next to Tabitha's chair.

"Put that in your backpack, please," she tells Tabitha. "You'll need it for your homework this weekend."

Tabitha quickly puts the study guide in her backpack.

"No! It's not hers!" I say. "It's Seth's!"

Humphrey squeaks at me. I don't understand him, but I can tell that he knows something I don't know.

I think Humphrey has some kind of plan. I don't know if it will work, but he's trying.

Tabitha should try like Humphrey. Maybe I should, too.

I am looking forward to spending a nice, quiet weekend in Room 26 when Tabitha's mom comes to take Humphrey home for the weekend.

"Carol, say hello to Og," Tabitha says, pulling her toward my tank. "He's so funny and cool. Can we take him home, too?"

"Humphrey travels better," Mrs. Brisbane says. "Og's tank is heavier, and he needs to have the temperature controlled. Taking care of him is a little more challenging than taking care of Humphrey."

Personally, I like a challenge. But I think Mrs. Brisbane is trying to keep me safe, and I appreciate that.

It's been a thrilling day—even more exciting than a water moccasin wrestling match back in the swamp!

But I'm surprised to see that Humphrey looks a little sad as he's carried out of Room 26. Is his squeak a good-bye to me? Or is it a thank-you?

Magic in the Air

· · · · · · · · · · · · · · · · ·

RUM-RUM. RUM-RUM. RUM-RUM. RUM-RUM! There they go, the bully bullfrogs again . . . bellowing away like they do every evening. Really, they give frogs a bad name! They also give me a big fat headache! I wish they'd just go away. Instead, I'm the one who went away—but I didn't mean to!

Oops. I nodded off again. It is soooo quiet with no bullfrogs here and my neighbor gone for the weekend. Total peace and quiet. Ah, the swamp was never like this.

I am content to float in the water. After a while, I break into song—a tune that Uncle Chinwag taught me:

> I sing a hoppy frog song,
> I sing my song out loud
> So everybody hears me
> And knows that I am proud!

I sing because I'm happy,
I sing because I'm sad,
I sing because it feels good
And that makes me so glad.

I sing a hoppy frog song
With jolly words that rhyme,
And since you like my frog song,
I'll sing it one more time!

It's a song without any end, so I sing many verses until Aldo comes in to clean.

"Hiya, Og, old pal," he greets me. "I heard you all the way down the hall."

He's friendly as usual, but he seems lost in thought as he does his work and leaves quickly.

The room is beautifully clean. No muck, no mud, no cattails, no pond scum.

I spend a very quiet evening and go to sleep early.

But in the morning, when the sunbeams warm my tank, it's back to my workouts. After all, as Granny Greenleaf says, "Be strong, live long."

Which is true . . . unless a wily water moccasin catches you off guard.

My morning is spent splashing and leaping. Once I leap so high, I touch the lid of my tank. That's a first!

I do more jumping jacks than I've ever done before (though I always miss my pal Jack when I do them).

I stop to give my muscles a break, and I am SHOCKED when the door to Room 26 opens and a mysterious figure who looks as wide as she is tall comes in.

"Og! Are you all right?" a familiar voice asks.

It's Mrs. Brisbane, all bundled up for cold weather. She hurries over to my tank.

"I couldn't sleep a wink last night. All I could think about was how cold it was. And I know that when the temperature drops, frogs go into hibernation!"

"I'm just fine!" I tell her, bouncing up and down to show her I'm not hibernating.

"Oh, Og! Thank goodness!" she says. "The students love to watch you and listen to you, and they'd be so disappointed and worried if you started hibernating."

Really? Disappointed and worried?

Hibernation is really just a nice, cozy nap, but I'd hate to miss out on all the activity in Room 26.

I want to see if Gail and Heidi make up and if Tabitha makes more friends.

I want to see if Mandy stops complaining—at least a little bit.

I want to hear more jokes from Kirk and Mr. Brisbane.

And I'm very curious to see what wacky thing my funny, furry neighbor, Humphrey, does next!

Ah, life at the Brisbanes' house! What more can any creature ask for?

Mr. Brisbane generously feeds me a cricket while his wife is out of the room.

I am busily digesting my treat . . . but when Mrs. Brisbane starts talking about me, I start to feel queasy.

"I found someone from the university to help us sort out this idea that Og should go back to the swamp," she tells her husband.

"What do you think he'll say?" Mr. Brisbane wonders.

"*She*," Mrs. Brisbane says. "I really don't know. Whatever she suggests, some students are bound to be disappointed." She sighs.

"You worry about Room Twenty-six too much," Mr. Brisbane says.

"I can't help it. But the good news is, Tabitha is getting more comfortable in class," Mrs. Brisbane tells her husband. "She and Seth have something in common. They both love sports."

Unlike Humphrey and me, Tabitha and Seth speak the same language. I hope they'll be friends, too.

"And Mandy is complaining less," she says. "Thanks to Og!"

"I'm trying," I tell her.

"Gail and Heidi are still at war, though," Mrs. Brisbane continues. "I thought they'd make up by now."

Mr. Brisbane pats her hand. "They'll have to work this out themselves, Sue."

Just like Granny Greenleaf, Mrs. Brisbane is always thinking about her tads.

She looks so sad, I hop up and down on my rock. "Don't worry, Mrs. B!" I shout. "Problems have a way of working themselves out."

I'm just repeating what Granny Greenleaf said. The Brisbanes chuckle and turn their attention to watching me.

I try to be as interesting as possible.

Later that night, I think about what Mrs. Brisbane said about Tabitha and Seth. The Brisbanes want them to be friends . . . and so do I.

And—hold on! Maybe Humphrey does, too. Could that be why he moved Seth's study guide? He must have wanted Tabitha to have them both so maybe they'd have to get together over the weekend.

That would be a pretty bold and smart plan. I wonder if it worked.

If it did, I feel pretty hopping good about having helped him, at least a little bit.

Then, my thoughts turn to the "she" from the university who is going to help the big tads decide whether I go or stay.

I'm still not sure what to wish for.

If I stay, I'm stuck in a tank. Plus, I have a "job" as a classroom pet that I don't completely understand yet.

If I go, it's back to beaky birds, wily water snakes and sneaky snapping turtles, or even worse, a painful shortage of food!

On Monday, I watch carefully to see if anything changed over the weekend.

When Heidi sticks her tongue out at Gail (who returns the gesture), I know nothing has changed there.

But Tabitha and Seth laugh and talk before class starts.

"Thanks for inviting me over," Seth says. "I'm glad you got my study guide. That was an awesome basketball game."

"Yes . . . and I hope we both get A's on the test," Tabitha replies.

So they *did* get together over the weekend. Humphrey's plan worked! (With a tiny bit of help from me.)

I see that another one of Humphrey's plans worked later in the week when Aldo comes in way before it's time to clean the classroom. Then I remember that he's supposed to teach a lesson.

I can't really make head or tail out of what he's doing with little squares of paper and the big tads running around looking at things in the classroom—even me.

That gives me plenty of time to dive and swim laps.

Later, I'm hoppy to hear Mrs. Brisbane tell Aldo, "You are a born teacher."

He and his mustache burst into a great big smile.

As the week goes on, I pay a little more attention to the other things Humphrey does to help the big tads.

When Gail and Heidi talk to him (not together, of course), he listens sympathetically to each of them. And when Art stares out the window instead of listening in class, Humphrey squeaks at him until he pays attention again. When Mrs. Brisbane calls on him, Art actually knows the answer!

He even helps the grown-ups. Humphrey offers very encouraging squeaks when Aldo seems worried, and he always seems to cheer up Mrs. Brisbane.

I have to admit, he helps *me* by waking me up when there's something important happening in the classroom.

And each evening, he opens that cage door and comes over to squeak at me.

At least I used to think he squeaked *at* me. Now I realize he's squeaking *to* me.

He can't understand me, but Humphrey always *tries*.

Pretty soon, I realize I'm trying to be more helpful, too. Especially when Tabitha talks to me—which is every single day.

"Og? Did you hear that song Mrs. Brisbane sang to me?" she asks one day.

"BOING-BOING! I sure did!" I reply.

"I think I found a new silver friend," she says. "Seth is pretty nice, for a boy."

"BING-BANG-BOING!" I agree.

After she returns to her chair, I'm a little low. I have lots of gold friends—my old friends in the swamp, like Jumpin' Jack, Silly Gilly and Uncle Chinwag.

I'd like to keep my new silver friends, too.

So I sing Mrs. Brisbane's song.

BOING-BOING-BOING,
BOING BOING BOING BO-ING!
BOING BOING BOING-BOING
BOING BOING BOING BOING BOING!

Before the other students come back into Room 26, Mrs. Brisbane tells Tabitha a secret. "No one knows it yet, but we're about to have a really special visitor," she says.

I guess she forgot that *I* know about the surprise guest, too. I just don't know what she'll think of me.

Call the Doctor

· · · · · · · · · · · · · · · · ·

Try harder, Granny Greenleaf tells me. "Don't climb the rock—jump over it! You can do it." But I'm just a little tad, and I can't jump very high yet. "Use a little leg power. You won't hop high unless you try," she says.

"I'll try," I promise.

I'm used to having guests in Room 26. Parents come into the classroom sometimes, and of course, Aldo comes every night during the week.

Sometimes Principal Morales drops in, always wearing a different tie.

But on this day, a total stranger comes into the room. It's our surprise visitor!

Mrs. Brisbane prepares us for this unusual event first. "Class, since we are dealing with the issue of whether Og belongs in the classroom—"

That gets my attention, and I'm afraid I let out an extra-loud "BOING!"

I'm waiting to hear Humphrey's excited squeaks, but he's

still in his little house, sleeping. I guess I would be, too, after the long workout he had on the wheel.

Mrs. Brisbane laughs. "That got Og's attention! Anyway, I decided to bring in an expert—a herpetologist from the university."

"Her-pa—what?" That's A.J. in his loud voice.

"Herpetologist," Mrs. Brisbane patiently explains. "A person who studies amphibians like Og, and reptiles like snakes."

Some of the big tads say, "Oooh!"

"Way to go!" I shout. I never heard of a herpetologist before, but I like this human already.

Mrs. Brisbane continues. "The herpetologist will talk to us about releasing captured frogs into the wild. We need more information before we make a decision," Mrs. Brisbane continues. "And Dr. Okeke is an expert."

"Oh-kay-kee?" Richie repeats. "What's that?"

"It's an African name," Mrs. Brisbane says.

"I like saying it," Richie replies. "Okeke."

"I *know* what he'll say." Heidi is very sure of herself. "He'll say Og belongs in the swamp with his friends and family."

"You don't know that," Gail declares.

They glare at each other.

"Dr. Okeke is a *she*. A woman," Mrs. Brisbane says. "Let's hear what she has to say."

The door opens, and a smiling woman wearing big round glasses enters. "Are you ready for me now?" she asks.

"*I* certainly am!" I answer. After all, I'm more interested in meeting a herpetologist than anyone else is.

"Ah! Our *Rana clamitans*," Dr. Okeke says, walking toward my tank.

"We call him Og," A.J. explains.

I hear a rather poor imitation of a boing, and I realize right away that it's Kirk.

Mrs. Brisbane gives him the kind of look that quiets him down.

Dr. Okeke leans down and peers into my tank. Her glasses make her eyes look unusually large, for a human.

"He's a fine specimen," she says. "A very handsome frog!"

"Thank you," I answer politely.

"And you say he came from McKenzie's Marsh?" she asks.

Mrs. Brisbane nods. "That's what we've been told."

"He was frognapped from his friends and family!" Heidi blurts out.

"But he *loves* Room Twenty-six," Gail says. "And we love him!"

Yeah—they love me so much, they want to send me back!

"He came to us from another classroom," Mrs. Brisbane explains. "We're not sure what we should do."

Dr. Okeke stops staring at me—thank goodness, as I was feeling a little edgy.

"Ideally, the best place to get a pet frog is to buy it from a dealer who raises them," she tells the class.

"Yes, but it's a little late for that," Mrs. Brisbane replies.

"What you should know is that frogs in the wild are rapidly disappearing," she says. "That's a huge global concern."

I'll say it's a big concern! Where are they disappearing to?

"What's happening to them?" Sayeh asks. She's so shy, I'm surprised she spoke.

"Diseases, new predators coming into their habitats, pollution in their water. In many places, their habitats are being destroyed by building houses," Dr. Okeke says. "In order to slow their decline, in some places it's absolutely illegal to take frogs out of the wild."

Here I was worried that I'd end up in jail, but now I'm afraid Mrs. Brisbane will end up in jail! Austin March's grandfather surely will be locked up.

"My advice is that you should never buy or adopt a frog if you don't know where it came from," the herpetologist continues.

"That's good advice," Mrs. Brisbane says. "But what about taking him back now?"

"It may be safe to release a frog *if* you release it to its place of birth," Dr. Okeke continues. "But Og may have picked up human germs here in the classroom that could affect the other creatures back in McKenzie's Marsh. It could wipe out an entire population near his home."

Who . . . me? I'd never do a thing like that, if I could help it.

Home. My heart feels a little tug.

Home is where Granny Greenleaf and Uncle Chinwag and Jumpin' Jack live. Home is full of crickets and dragonflies and other yummy bugs.

But home also has hungry enemies, like birds with large beaks.

Still, there's no place like home.

But what if I have picked up something that would harm my friends and family? What if *they* all disappeared and I was to blame?

Richie suddenly jumps up and stands by his desk. "He's our pet! We love him!"

Gail also rises to her feet. "What would happen to him back in the marsh? He could be . . . eaten!" She shudders.

I shudder, too, because it's true.

"But he's *wild*," Garth insists. "He should live out in nature."

"Should we all go live in caves? Because humans used to live out in nature, too." That's a surprising comment from Art.

Art may not always pay attention, but he is smart.

"But his *friends*. And *family*. He must miss them so much!" Heidi has tears in her eyes.

"You see our problem," Mrs. Brisbane tells Dr. Okeke.

The herpetologist nods. "I do. But be careful not to think of animals as if they are human. They don't necessarily think and feel the way we do. And life in the swamp isn't easy."

That's the truth! Have you ever stared a snapping turtle in the face? Or been hungry for a long, long time? Even though I'm cold-blooded, that thought gives me a chill.

"Most wild animals don't stay with their families," Dr. Okeke says. "Many of you have pets that have left their parents and brothers and sisters."

Everyone in the classroom is silent.

"There are other options," Dr. Okeke says. "There's a local wildlife center I work with called Piney Woods."

"Oh! I've been there! It's cool!" A.J. says.

Dr. Okeke nods. "It *is* cool. There are nature hikes, and we have an educational program with both indoor and outdoor exhibits. There are all kinds of animals there, from wolves to eagles. If you don't want to keep Og as a pet, he could find a nice home there . . . and help educate people about frogs."

Wolves? Eagles? I think I'd prefer to stay here with the big tads.

"But I think he should be in the *wild*!" Heidi says.

"I know," Dr. Okeke agrees. "That's why I mentioned this option. While he wouldn't be back with his friends and family, we would create a natural environment for him with grasses and water. So it would be more like the marsh. And he'd have more space."

The big tads are quiet for a moment.

"Could he hop around more?" Garth asks.

"Definitely," Dr. Okeke replies. "And hundreds of children like you could see him and learn about frogs and how endangered they are."

"Could *we* visit him there?" Sayeh asks.

"Of course!" Dr. Okeke nods. "Do you have any other questions about frogs?"

Gail giggles as she raises her hand. "If you kiss a frog, will it turn into a handsome prince?"

Dr. Okeke chuckles. "I can guarantee it will *not*. But it could make you feel a little sick. In fact, there are frogs that are deadly poisonous. Not Og, of course."

"I definitely am not!" I assure them. The very thought of it!

"He *peed* on me," Mandy blurts out. "And all I did was pick him up."

Dr. Okeke goes on to explain that frogs often urinate when they are picked up. "It's a natural defense against enemies."

"But I'm not Og's enemy," Mandy replies. "I think he's cute."

I think Mandy is cute, too, when she's not complaining.

"Og didn't know that," Dr. Okeke says. "How would you like it if a giant hand came down from the sky and picked you up?"

Mandy rolls her eyes and says, "I wouldn't."

After a few more questions, Mrs. Brisbane thanks Dr. Okeke. "You've given us a lot to think about," she tells her. "And we thank you for your time."

Before she leaves, Dr. Okeke passes out SAVE THE FROGS buttons. She even leans one up against my tank.

"Thank you!" I tell her.

"You're welcome, Og," she replies.

I hope humans will save the frogs. I hope my friends will save me!

Having a guest was special, but there was even more excitement in Room 26 at the end of the week.

The big tads are always chatting and laughing when they aren't studying. They're as full of energy as a lively swarm of flies back in the swamp. But on Friday, they are even more energetic than usual.

They're more like a billowing, buzzing swarm of locusts!

It takes me a while to figure out what's causing the hubbub, but there is a lot of talk about Richie's birthday party, which is coming up on Saturday.

We frogs don't have birthday parties, but our hatchday parties are loud, leaping, jump-for-joy celebrations.

It sounds as if Richie's will be one, too. He's invited all the big tads, and he says there will be a magician to perform amazing tricks, like pulling a rabbit out of a hat! And that's just part of Richie's plans.

I couldn't help noticing that I didn't get an invitation, but neither did Humphrey.

So I am shocked right off my rock when Mrs. Brisbane

announces that Richie will be taking Humphrey home for the weekend. He gets to go to the party!

I have to say, Richie does ask Mrs. Brisbane if I can come, too.

I am hopeful, until she says I am going home with *her* instead. AND that her husband has a special surprise for me.

I think pulling a rabbit out of a hat would be a pretty good surprise, but I wonder what tricks Bert has up his sleeve.

Tanks a Lot!

. . . .

FLOATING. JUST FLOATING on a relaxing spring afternoon. My belly is full, the water is just right, and the peepers are singing their spring song. But what's that shadow ahead? I take a giant leap, and sneaky Chopper misses me—barely. So much for a relaxing day, but that's life in the swamp.

Luckily, life is more relaxing at my teacher's house this weekend.

My first night there is pleasant enough. I get a juicy cricket treat—thanks, Mr. Brisbane!

But there's nothing else I'd call *special*. What was Mrs. Brisbane talking about?

The next morning, the Brisbanes both go out in the car and leave me alone. I'm trying to imagine all the fun my friends are having at Richie's hatchday—I mean birthday—party, so I decide to take my mind off what I'm missing. I launch into my weekend workout: jumping jacks, push-ups and giant leaps, followed by energetic splashing.

I want to see if I can hit the lid again, and once, I succeed!

After a while, the Brisbanes return with armloads of bags and smiles on their faces.

"Og, we've got another treat for you!" Mr. Brisbane announces. "Thanks to Pet-O-Rama!"

Pet-O-Rama must be quite a place. It's where my tasty tidbits come from. Even Humphrey came from there, and I am a teensy bit jealous.

Mr. Brisbane wasn't kidding about a treat for me. He spends most of the day fixing up my tank.

When he's finished, the place looks pretty spiffy.

Now the dinky dish of water has been replaced and HALF of my tank is a lovely swimming pool. I'll be able to dive and swim! BING-BANG-*BOING*! I do love to make a splash!

And he's added some more leafy green plants. It's not exactly like the swamp, but it feels more like home.

Mr. Brisbane tops off this perfect day by feeding me *another* tasty cricket—while Mrs. Brisbane is out of the room, of course.

"You don't have to mention this to my wife," he tells me.

Believe me, I won't!

That night, when the house is quiet, I make up a new version of the hoppy frog song.

I sing a hoppy frog song,
I sing my song out loud.
I have a brand-new home now,
And I am feeling proud!

It's fun to dive and swim around,
I love my new plants, too.
And to my friends the Brisbanes:
I really do thank you!

And when I'm feeling a little tired and ready to doze off, I think that Mr. and Mrs. Brisbane wouldn't go to so much trouble if they were really planning to send me to Piney Woods.

Would they?

I'm pretty excited about returning to Room 26 on Monday. I hope that my neighbor, Humphrey, will notice the changes in my tank.

He doesn't . . . at first. And neither do any of the other big tads. They're too busy chattering away about the party like a crowd of cackling crows.

From what I hear, somehow Humphrey ended up being pulled out of the magician's hat. I wish I could ask the little guy how *that* happened.

I notice other things, too. Like the fact that Heidi and

Gail are best friends again. From the way they act, it's hard to believe they ever called each other names or stuck their tongues out at each other.

"Thanks for sticking up for me," Heidi says.

"I couldn't let that bully treat you that way," Gail answers. "After all, you're my friend."

I don't know who that bully was. Could it have been George?

I guess Granny Greenleaf was right about problems having a way of working themselves out. Heidi and Gail are truly gold friends.

The fact that they've made up is more magical than pulling a hamster out of a hat!

Then my neighbor notices the changes in my tank and lets out a series of excited squeaks.

The big tads notice, too.

"Whoa, Oggy the Frog! That's some snazzy swimming pool you've got there!" A.J. says as he leans down to inspect my tank.

The other students gather around.

"Now he can dive and swim," Sayeh says softly. "He could be in the Olympics."

"Or the Froglympics," Kirk adds.

"And his tank seems a lot more swampy with all those new plants," Miranda says.

"I think he needs some furniture," Richie suggests. "Like a bed and a couch."

Gail giggles. "And a TV!"

"How about a FIREPLACE?" A.J. hollers.

The bed and the TV sound nice. The fireplace—no, thank you!

Later, when the students leave Room 26 for home, Humphrey doesn't waste any time in flinging open the door to his cage and scampering over to take a closer peek at my tank.

"Watch this!" I stand on my tippy toes on my rock and then leap into the swimming area with a giant, splashy dive. It's a dive any frog would be proud of.

But is Humphrey impressed?

No way! The little guy panics and rushes back to his cage.

Oops! I forgot that hamsters shouldn't get wet. I'll try not to splash him in the future. I don't want to upset him.

❧ ❧ ❧ ❧

When Aldo comes in to clean, he has two surprises for me.

One is a treat: a mealworm. Thanks, Aldo.

He also notices my new and improved tank right away and thinks it's awesome. "A frog like you deserves a swimming pool," he says. "Now you can dive and leap as much as you want."

"BOING-BOING!" I agree.

The second surprise is that he tells me he has applied to college and was accepted.

That's what the piece of paper was all about, and he turned it in!

"Humphrey here found out at the party, but I wanted you to know, too, Og," he says.

"Way to go!" I tell him, bouncing up and down on my rock.

It's a hoppy celebration, something like a hatchday.

I feel very contented for most of the week.

I'm almost glad there are no more surprises. I can just think. Float. Doze. *Be.*

But on Thursday afternoon, suddenly Heidi shouts, "Look! Out the window—look!"

I hop up and down on my rock so I can get a good view.

Curtains of fluffy white flakes are falling from the sky, and the ground is already getting white as well.

"It's snowing!" some of the students shout.

I've seen a few white puffs fall from the sky before but nothing like this. When it's cold enough for the white stuff, it's time for me to take a long, long nap.

"Boy, I've never seen it snow so hard in my whole life," Richie says.

Neither have I. I've never appreciated the quiet beauty of snow piling up. In the past, I've slept right through it.

My poor friends back in the swamp are probably sound asleep right now and missing this sight.

There is something to be said for being a classroom pet. Regular meals, no enemies, and now—snow!

Mrs. Brisbane helps her students get bundled up at the end of the day.

"See you tomorrow," she tells us when she hurries out the door.

That's what she always says . . . at least during the week.

The little guy next door just sits in his cage, staring out at the curtains of snow filling the empty parking lot.

He looks and looks . . . but Aldo's car never arrives.

Aldo never misses an evening of work. Maybe he's hibernating.

Outside, the whole world is white: Who knew this could happen?

There's nothing out there except snow.

And more snow.

Very, very cold snow.

All that cold snow makes me feel very . . . very . . . sleepy.

It snows a lot more all night, and the next day, *no one* shows up for class—not even Mrs. Brisbane!

My little neighbor must have realized that nobody is coming to school because he flings open the door of his cage and stares out the window for a long, long time.

I sleep quite a bit, but when the bell rings for recess or

lunch, I wake up. With no big tads making noise, I quickly drop back to sleep.

In the afternoon, I sleep more deeply, dreaming of the time that Jumpin' Jack and I played a game of leapfrog, hopping over each other, and Jack landed nose to nose with a hungry-looking raccoon.

I've never seen a frog leap backward so far and so fast!

Scritch-scritch-scritch!

No animal in the swamp goes "scritch!"

I'm awake now, and the sound is Humphrey writing in his notebook.

It's not a bad sound, and I nod off again.

It's as chilly as a water moccasin's heart. I'm aware of some sounds—the last bell of the day, Humphrey spinning on his wheel—but mostly I doze.

Sometime during the night, a loud machine goes back and forth outside. A whirling orange light streams through the window.

The only other sound I hear all night is Humphrey squeaking right outside my tank. I wake up just enough to say good night.

Humphrey gives up and goes back to his cage. Room 26 is quieter than a water snake silently slithering through the dark water.

From Hero to Zero

·················

THE TEMPERATURE IS *falling rapidly. The swamp looks bleak. Most of the birds have flown away, and the green leaves are gone. My tummy is empty, my leaps are lower, my heart is slower. The days are shorter, and it gets colder and colder. It's time to find a place to burrow in so no one can see me . . . but I'm so, so sleepy.*

I snooze. I slumber. I dream.

But after a while, I leap up with a feeling of panic.

Humphrey hasn't been spinning on his wheel for a *long* time, and it's light outside now.

The last time I heard him squeak was hours ago, and now I remember what a weak squeak it was.

Suddenly, I get it. My brain's a little fuzzy, but I remember that Humphrey needs to eat a lot more often than I do. Is he really hungry? *Really hungry?*

If I just take a long nap, I'll be fine. Poor Humphrey needs food and water.

The furry guy always tries to help his fellow students, and he even helps giant tads like Aldo.

He has big plans in his little brain.

But I'm stuck in my tank. How can I help?

"Humphrey, are you all right?" I ask him.

It seems like a long time before I hear a sad and pitiful squeak.

Soon, Humphrey drags himself out of his cage. I think he's probably headed for my tank, but instead, he takes a turn and heads for the pile of food containers Mrs. Brisbane keeps on the table.

He *is* hungry, poor fellow.

He stops and looks up at the tall bags and jars of hamster food towering above him. But as tiny as he is, he *charges* at the huge bag of the little brown nuggets the tads feed Humphrey. I don't know what they are, but I'll bet they don't taste half as good as crickets.

"Be careful!" I tell him, but it's too late.

The bag wobbles back and forth and then—BAM! It crashes right down on Humphrey.

I hear him squeaking, so he must be okay, but he's trapped under the big bag. How in the swamp is a little critter like him going to get out?

I don't know how I can help. But at least I can try.

Almost without thinking, I say, "Help is on the way, Humphrey!"

But I don't have a door like Humphrey, and my tank has a cover. But wait! I've reached it a couple of times during my recent workouts. Maybe there's a chance . . .

So I hop.

And I leap.

And I jump.

I can almost hear Granny Greenleaf saying, "If at first you don't succeed, leap, leap again!"

I jump higher and higher until I finally touch it.

Then I leap even higher, and would you believe it? The top just pops right off.

With one more giant leap, I sail out of the tank and land on the tabletop!

I'm not one to brag, but my species, *Rana clamitans*, is noted for our impressive leaping abilities. And today, I may have outdone them all.

"I'm on my way, Humphrey! Don't worry!" I say.

I'm sure he's plenty worried, since all he hears is "BOING-BOING!"

Since leaping is my strong point, I can throw my entire body at the bag. But I have to be careful that it doesn't crush Humphrey. What I want to do is open up the space around him.

It's hard work, but let's face it, a bag of hamster food isn't as scary as a large-beaked bird.

"Get ready, Humphrey! I'm here!" I tell him.

I run at the bag and smack it again and again. I pretend it's Chopper, the mean old turtle, and I'm fighting for my life. Except it's Humphrey's life I'm fighting for.

The space gets bigger and bigger until I see an opening. But where is Humphrey?

By now, I'm so worked up, I've switched to my extreme danger call, which is "SCREE-SCREE!"

And then Humphrey staggers out into the open.

After all that wobbling back and forth, I'm afraid the bag might fall right back on the little guy.

"SCREEEEE!" I warn him.

And what do you know? Suddenly, Humphrey grabs onto my back.

I hop away as fast as I can with Humphrey clinging to me. The bag crashes down, barely missing us, but I keep on hopping.

It's just like a scene in a movie I saw on TV, where every-body rode horses. I don't know if anyone ever rode a frog before, but here we go!

"SCREEEE!" I shout. "Hang on, Humphrey!"

"SQUEAK-SQUEAK-SQUEAK!" he replies.

BING-BANG-BOING! I understand him perfectly.

Suddenly, all the lights come on! I stop hopping, and Humphrey slides down off my back.

Mrs. Brisbane, all bundled up in a heavy coat and hat, rushes over to our table. "How on earth did they get out?" she asks.

Mr. Morales is there, too, and they both seem pretty amazed to see us out of our cages.

Aldo rushes into the room, shouting, "Never fear, Aldo's here!"

All three of them are here because they've been worried about *us*.

Mrs. Brisbane puts Humphrey back in his cage and gives him some of those nuggets.

Mr. Morales returns me to my tank and gives me two lovely crickets. I'll bet George never had the principal feed *him*!

Soon, Miranda, Heidi, Garth, Sayeh and a bunch of other people arrive.

Everybody's been worried about us!

And then I wonder: What did George do the last few days? Was he cold or hungry?

"I checked Room Twenty-seven, and Miss Loomis must have taken George home on Thursday," Aldo says.

So George is safe to **RUM-RUM** as much as he likes!

The day has a very hoppy ending. Aldo leaves to go study for a test, but Mr. Morales helps Mrs. Brisbane take Humphrey and me to her home until school is back in session.

In the car, I hear Humphrey say, "SQUEAK-SQUEAK-SQUEAK!"

"Anytime, pal," I answer.

Back at the Brisbanes' house, Mr. Morales and Mrs. Brisbane manage to sort out what happened—except they think Humphrey got out because someone didn't close his cage door.

They don't know that he can open that door anytime he wants. He does it all the time! And he closes it again when he's back in the cage. But—frog's honor—I'll never tell.

"Maybe Og was trying to help Humphrey get food and managed to leap out of his tank," Mrs. Brisbane says.

"It's hard to believe," Mr. Morales agreed. "But it's the only answer."

Mrs. Brisbane turns to look at me. "You're a true hero, Og."

Humphrey squeaks. I'm pretty sure he agrees with her.

If I were a loudmouth bullfrog, I'd probably be bragging about what I did. Instead, I simply say, "No problem."

✦ ✦ ✦ ✦

Two days later, we're back in Room 26, and the snow is melting quickly under a sunny sky.

I'm proud and pleased when Mrs. Brisbane tells the whole class about my heroic deed.

A.J. loudly shouts, "Three cheers for Og!"

To my amazement, the whole class cries, "Hip hip hooray! Hip hip hooray! Hip hip hooray for Og!"

"SQUEAK-SQUEAK-SQUEAK!" my neighbor cheers with them.

He sounds pretty happy, but later, when we're alone, I wonder if Humphrey would have come to my rescue.

He couldn't move heavy things by himself, and he's too small for me to ride on his back. But if he could, would he save me? I just don't know.

There is no time to worry about that question during the week, because there's so much going on in Room 26.

Poems are written. Cards are made. Hearts are cut out of paper. Red paper hearts are strung across the chalkboards and on the bulletin board.

The cards are called valentines. The poems are for a poetry festival. I'm not sure what either of those things are, but I keep my eyes and ears open.

It turns out that Valentine's Day is a day when humans give each other cards and candy and heart-shaped things to show how much they care.

Even Humphrey and I receive valentines from the big tads.

My favorite is from Mandy.

Red is the rose,
Green is the frog.
I love my new friend.
His name is Og.

I know that sometimes I am a pain,
But he helps me to NOT complain!

Nobody ever said anything like that to me back in the swamp.

Nice.

All the big tads are excited because their parents are coming in the afternoon to hear the poems.

While my friends are at lunch, I take time to daydream. But my concentration is broken when I hear Humphrey scribbling like crazy in his little notebook.

What in the swamp could he be writing?

Whatever it is, he uses his teeth to tear the page out of his tiny notebook. He even reads it aloud.

Squeak-squeak-squeak-squeak,
Squeak squeak-squeak-squeak,
Squeak-squeak-squeak squeak,
Squeak squeak, squeak squeak!

Too bad I can't understand a word of it!

Next, he swings his cage door open, and I glance at the clock.

"They're coming back any minute," I try to warn him.

I guess he understands, because as fast as I've ever seen him move, he slides down the table leg, races to Mrs.

Brisbane's desk, drops the paper on the floor, and scurries back up onto the table.

If no one notices it this afternoon, Aldo will probably just sweep it away!

Once Humphrey is safely back in his cage and our class-mates come back in the room, I keep a close eye on that paper.

And I'm very relieved when Mrs. Brisbane picks it up!

It's fun to see the parents of the big tads arrive later in the day. Most of them come over to our table to say hi to Humphrey and me.

The big tads do a good job reading their poems. And if they get stuck, Mrs. Brisbane gives them a little help.

A funny thing happens near the end of the day. Mrs. Brisbane reaches in her pocket and takes out that ragged scrap of paper Humphrey left on the floor. She explains that she found it and says, "It expresses the feelings the children in this room have for each other."

I listen very carefully as she reads.

A friend doesn't have to be a work of art,
Just have a heart.
A friend doesn't need to have fur or hair
To care.

A friend doesn't have a thing to do
But like you.
A friend doesn't need to say a word
To be heard.
It's not so hard to be a friend
In the end.

Humphrey wrote that? I like it a lot, even though it gives me a funny feeling in my stomach because I think he wrote that poem about me.

And if he did, I guess the little fellow and I are truly friends. I don't think that could happen back in the swamp, where amphibians and mammals are never friends.

But it's just the kind of thing that happens all the time in Room 26.

For a cold-blooded frog, I feel awfully warm inside.

Later that night, I think about all the nice things the big tads—and Humphrey—wrote about me. So I write a poem, too. I don't have a notebook, but I write it in my head.

Of all the places I get my kicks,
My favorite (so far) is Room Twenty-six.
To my human friends, I just want to say,
I wish you a happy Valentine's Day.

> *I never thought I'd be friends with a hamster,*
> *But now I am—of that, I am sure.*

There! I didn't *exactly* rhyme something with hamster—but I came pretty close! I think that's good enough to be on a heart-shaped card.

I sleep peacefully that night, knowing that my friends in Mrs. Brisbane's class love me as much as I love them.

On Monday, Mrs. Brisbane makes an announcement, and I am bowled over.

"Students, it is time for us to come to some kind of agreement about Og's future. You've heard what Dr. Okeke had to say. Tomorrow we will be holding a debate on why you think Og should stay in Room Twenty-six or be moved to the wildlife center at Piney Woods."

"SQUEAK!" Humphrey scrambles to the front of his cage. "SQUEAK-SQUEAK-SQUEAK!"

The little guy sure is excited.

"SQUEAK-SQUEAK-SQUEAK!" he repeats.

I realize this is the first time he's heard about Piney Woods. "You were sleeping when Dr. Okeke was here before," I tell him. I sure wish I could speak Hamster.

Mrs. Brisbane asks Mandy to pass out sheets outlining the assignment.

"The questions on this worksheet will help you figure

out the pros and cons of Og going to Piney Woods," she explains. "What do you feel would be best for Og and for everyone in our class and why?"

"SQUEAK-SQUEAK-SQUEAK!" Humphrey shouts.

"Settle down, Humphrey," Mrs. Brisbane says, then turns back to the class. "After you answer all of the questions, I want you to prepare your arguments. After the debate, we will take a vote and decide once and for all."

She doesn't bat an eyelid. Her lips don't quiver.

Does *she* want me to leave Room 26?

Do they *all* want me to leave Room 26?

Do *I* have no say in it? (Well, it's clear that I *don't*.)

I feel a bit dizzy.

Just last week I thought I was a hero, but right now I feel like a total zero.

The Great Frog Debate

· · · · · · · · · · · · · · · · ·

THE SWAMP IS still cold, but I'm waking up. Everything looks different, and I don't see anyone I know. Where are Granny Greenleaf and Uncle Chinwag? Where's my pal Jumpin' Jack? They must be sleeping somewhere. Isn't anyone awake? Then I hear them.

We are the bullfrogs, defenders of the swamp!
We are the bullfrogs, mightier than all!
Bullfrogs reign! Bullfrogs rule!
RUM-RUM! RUM-RUM! RUM-RUM!

Help! They're surrounding me! Can't somebody get me out of here?!

I'm not sorry to wake up from that daydream. It was a little bit too real.

Room 26 isn't as noisy as the swamp was in my dream, but there's tension in the air as the big tads prepare for the Great Frog Debate. That's what they're calling it.

I'm as worried as a bullfrog who's lost his voice. I'm as edgy as a duck stuck in the muck.

What I'm trying to say is: I am nervous. And so are the big tads. Even Mrs. Brisbane seems a little anxious today.

And Humphrey? He's squeaked so much already, I'm afraid he's going to lose his voice!

"SQUEAK-SQUEAK-SQUEAK-*SQUEAK*!"

I dive into the water side of my tank and try to Float. Doze. *Be.* It's not working today.

Sayeh's nose is about two inches from a piece of paper she's been studying, while Heidi is talking to herself.

Gail's not giggling at *all.* And when A.J. greets me with his usual "Hi, Oggy!" his voice is much softer than usual.

Garth cleans his glasses over and over.

Mandy frowns. She looks over at me, but for once, I can't make her smile.

I don't feel much like smiling, either.

Tabitha stares into space, looking glum. When I say, "Cheer up!" she doesn't even glance my way.

I look around my cozy tank with its clean pool of water . . . the lovely green moss . . . my rock.

Miranda, Richie and Seth all toss Froggy Fish Sticks into my tank when Mrs. Brisbane isn't looking. I don't eat them all, because if I'm going back to the swamp, I have to be in lean shape for jumping. Besides, I'm really not hungry.

After taking attendance, Mrs. Brisbane sends the tads

off to gym first thing in the morning. I have no idea what they do there. But when they get back, she tells the class that instead of our regular subjects, we'll start with the debate.

That's good, because I don't think my friends could think about anything else this morning. I know the last thing on *my* mind is math.

If amphibians like me could sweat, I'd be sweating.

The worst part is, *I'm* not even sure what my fate should be!

When Mrs. Brisbane says, "Let the Great Frog Debate begin," my fabulous leaping legs suddenly feel all wobbly.

"Let us start with a speaker on the side of Og moving to Piney Woods," she says.

A lot of hands go up. Even Heidi, who usually forgets to raise her hand, is waving hers in the air. Naturally, Mrs. Brisbane calls on her.

Heidi has notes written on a piece of paper. She has a very determined look on her face, but her hands are shaking and the paper is, too.

"It's not that I don't love Og, because I *do,*" she begins. She glances over at my tank. "I truly do, Og."

That's a very good beginning.

"But he was stolen from his home in McKenzie's Marsh . . . and that might even be *illegal,*" she says.

"I checked, and it's not illegal here," Mrs. Brisbane interrupts her.

"Well, it should be!" Heidi replies. "It's wrong to take a

small, helpless creature away from his family and friends. Away from his *enbironment*."

"Environment," Mrs. Brisbane corrects her.

I'm still thinking about the *small, helpless creature* part. Maybe the bullfrogs think of me that way, but I believe I am an extraordinary leaper, jumper and helper to all green frogs!

"If you were taken from your home, it would be called kidnapping," Heidi tells the class.

I look at the faces of the other big tads, and they are very serious.

"I wish Og could go back to McKenzie's Marsh. But since he might make his friends sick, he should go to Piney Woods, where he can be in his own . . . *environment*," Heidi continues. But I see her lip quiver a bit. "Even though I'll really miss you, Og!"

She quickly sits down, and Mrs. Brisbane calls on someone who is for keeping me in Room 26.

"I think Og is super cool," A.J. bellows. "I think he should stay here because he can teach us a lot."

"Would you like to tell us more about what Og can teach us?" our teacher asks.

A.J. hesitates. "Like, what amphibians are like and, um, what it's like to be cold-blooded. And, um . . . he's so funny when he goes 'BOING.'"

He sits down quickly, just like Heidi did.

At Piney Woods, I think that I'd be fed, I'd get to be outdoors, and I'd have a bigger space to hop around. I wouldn't have any enemies, and lots of people would see how cool a green frog can be.

In Room 26, I have no enemies, everybody loves me, I can help the big tads and Mrs. Brisbane, and I have a new furry friend.

Humphrey breaks my concentration with some alarmingly loud squeaks. "SQUEAK-SQUEAK-SQUEAK!!!!"

"Thanks for your opinion, Humphrey," Mrs. Brisbane says. I think she's trying not to laugh.

And so it goes. Garth rambles on about how animals should never be taken from the wild and why.

"But Og has already been taken from the wild," Mrs. Brisbane says. "So now what?"

Garth mumbles, "Piney Woods," and sits down.

When Mrs. Brisbane asks Tabitha, she stares down at her desk and doesn't say anything. I think I see tears in her eyes. Has she changed her mind?

Gail is all for keeping me in Room 26. "Because he's cute and we love him and I can tell he likes it here."

It's a short answer, but she's right. I do like Room 26. I like the big tads and Mrs. Brisbane. I like my new, clean tank and having a variety of interesting things to eat.

Despite the fact that I peed on her, Mandy thinks I should stay, because I make her feel cheerier! That's nice, especially coming from her.

Richie's speech is short and sweet. "We took in Og as

our classroom pet. We shouldn't get rid of him. That's just rude."

Seth agrees. "Og makes Room Twenty-six more fun. And he's good company for Humphrey!"

"I think he's cool, too," Kirk says next. "I want him to stay, but I wonder if that's selfish. Is he happy here? Would he be happier at Piney Woods?"

Kirk hesitates, and I feel a joke coming on. "And why are frogs so happy?" he asks. "Because they eat whatever bugs them."

All the big tads groan, and Mrs. Brisbane tells Kirk to sit down.

"Sayeh?" Mrs. Brisbane says. "I think you were in favor of returning Og to the swamp. Where do you stand on Piney Woods?"

Sayeh stands up and hesitates before she speaks. She doesn't have any notes.

I just hope that whatever she says, she speaks loudly enough so we can hear her.

"Yes, Mrs. Brisbane. I agreed with Heidi that Og was stolen away from his home and his family and friends. It seemed wrong to me, because it wasn't his choice."

Heidi gives Sayeh a thumbs-up sign.

Sayeh swallows hard and continues. "But I have been thinking a lot about my life. I had a home in a different country. My family and friends were there. And then we moved here, to a faraway place that was very different. We had to leave other family members and friends behind."

All the big tads are very quiet. Even Kirk looks serious for once.

"Like Og, it wasn't my idea to move," Sayeh continues. "My parents said we must leave. It was the hardest thing I've ever done. This was a strange place, but soon I had new friends and I liked this new country. I don't know when it happened, but after a while, *this* became home. I still think of my old home, but this is where I want to live now. It is my true home."

Sayeh stops and looks toward my tank.

"And I can't help wondering if this is how it is for Og. Of course, he loved the swamp and his friends and family. But every day, he seems more at home in Room 26. He hops and leaps and makes us laugh. And his great, loud boings remind me to speak up for myself."

"BOING-BOING-BOING-BOING!" I agree. Because this is the best speech I've ever heard. And I helped Sayeh, and I didn't even know it!

The room has been very quiet, but there are a few nervous laughs when I chime in.

Then Humphrey pipes up with a "SQUEAK-SQUEAK-SQUEAK-SQUEAK!" and my friends burst out laughing.

"All right, class," Mrs. Brisbane says with a smile. "Let Sayeh finish."

"Thank you, Og, for helping me. I have changed my mind. I think he should stay." Sayeh sits down.

I can tell she's glad to be finished.

"Thank you, Sayeh!" I say. "BOING-BOING! You have helped me make up my mind."

Because I know where my home really is.

There is great silence in the classroom. Even Humphrey is quiet.

Suddenly, Tabitha jumps up. "Og helped me, too! This has been a strange place for me, but Og made me feel at home. I don't know how he did it, but he made me feel like trying. I'm sorry I didn't say it sooner, but I really want him to stay! And I hope all my new friends in Room Twenty-six agree!"

"I agree!" I tell her, and she smiles.

"Thank you for speaking up, Tabitha. Anyone else?" Mrs. Brisbane asks, looking around the room. "Art?"

"Once I kind of dozed off and Og woke me up before I got in trouble," Art says. Then he adds, "Sorry, Mrs. Brisbane."

"I'll pay more attention next time." She laughs. "Og helped me, too."

I did, didn't I? I made her life easier by liking the mealworms, and I helped get Mrs. Brisbane's attention so she saw that paper Aldo was so worried about.

It's true! I'm doing my part as a classroom pet. Now, if only I can keep my job.

"Thanks to all of you who spoke," Mrs. Brisbane says. "The lunch bell will ring at any moment. I want each of you to write your decision on one of these slips of paper." She walks around the room handing them out.

"BOING!" She didn't give me one. Or Humphrey.

"Write 'Piney Woods' or 'Room Twenty-six,' fold it, and put it in the box by the door on your way out," Mrs. Brisbane continues. "Do not put your name on it. This is a secret vote."

I see my friends writing, but I can't tell what they're jotting down.

The bell rings, and one by one, the big tads file out, each dropping a vote into the box.

"Thank you," Mrs. Brisbane tells them as they leave. "I will count the votes when we get back from lunch."

Some of the big tads groan. "Can't you count them now?" A.J. asks.

"After lunch," Mrs. Brisbane says firmly.

They all leave the room, and Humphrey quickly opens his cage door—and just as quickly closes it again.

I see why. Mrs. Brisbane has come back into the classroom. "Now, where did I leave my lunch?" she asks. I don't answer, because I think she's talking to herself.

Humphrey stares at her intently as she rummages through her handbag, and then through another large bag she carries with her.

"I'd forget my head if it wasn't attached," she mumbles.

I wouldn't like to see a headless teacher!

Then she starts opening all of the desk drawers and searches them.

There's still no lunch, so she flings open the closet door and disappears from view. I can hear her muttering to herself.

When she comes out, she says, "I know I made my lunch this morning. And then I put it in—" She stops suddenly. "I put it in the *car*! Oh, and now I'll hardly have time to eat it."

She rushes out again.

Humphrey and I are all alone again. It's just us and that ballot box in Room 26.

I stare at the box, knowing my fate will be decided by the slips of paper inside.

I'm feeling so jumpy, I hardly notice Humphrey open his cage door and skitter across the table. But as I realize he's sliding down the table leg, I am very nervous.

"Humphrey! Don't go! You won't have time to get back to your cage!" I tell him.

He darts across the room—and what's that he has in his mouth? A tiny slip of paper.

"Come back!" I shout. But Humphrey keeps going.

The box sits on a stool. It's a lot lower than our table, but it's very tall for a small hamster to climb.

So I am amazed that Humphrey neatly climbs the rungs of the stool and—with great effort—pulls himself up onto the top.

"Careful, Humphrey!" I tell him.

Then he stands on his tippy toes and hangs on to the rim of the box with one paw. He drops the paper into the box with the others.

The box teeters a little and starts to tip.

"Watch out!" I scream, and give my danger warning. "SCREEE!"

Humphrey quickly lets go and slides down to the top of the stool. Just as he slides down one leg, the bell rings.

Lunchtime is over!

"HURRY!" I shout. "SCREEE! SCREEE!" I just can't help myself.

He races across the room as fast as a jackrabbit, grabs the cord to the blinds and starts swinging.

"Hurry, Humphrey!" I tell him. "Please!"

The door opens and students stream into Room 26 just as Humphrey lands on the table and speeds toward his cage.

My heart is pounding even faster than his footsteps as he runs into the cage and closes the door before anyone— except me—notices.

"You did it!" I tell him. "YOU DID IT!"

My neighbor weakly answers with a squeak.

Decision Time

· · · · · · · · · · · · · · · ·

PLOP. PLOP. PLOP-PLOP. It's raining. Plop. Plop. Plop-plop. Squeak-squeak-squeak! I'm in my cozy tank in Room 26, and I'm here because I'm a classroom pet who helps my friends, just like Humphrey. I can Float. Doze. Be. And I only get wet when I want to. Because I'm here to stay.

Too bad it's just a daydream. The sound of the raindrops on the windows of Room 26 usually calms me, but since this is the day the class is voting on my future, I'm not a bit relaxed, and neither are the big tads.

Humphrey's been spinning his wheel nonstop. The poor guy will be exhausted!

All of the big tads are restless, too. It's time to count the votes, but Mrs. Brisbane is waiting for one person to arrive.

One person? Is it Bert? Is it Dr. Okeke?

Nope. But it's someone very important: Mr. Morales, the principal. This time, he is wearing a tie with little frogs all over it. They look a lot like me!

"I decided to have someone from outside Room Twenty-six tally up the votes," Mrs. Brisbane tells the class.

Before he begins, Mr. Morales says, "Mrs. Brisbane told me you all put a lot of thought into your votes. So now . . . we'll find out the final decision."

Final decision.

Go or stay.

We love you or we don't.

You're in or you're out.

There is no in-between.

But at least I know what I'm hoping for. I hope the vote is for me to stay. Because Humphrey and the big tads have taught me what a good classroom pet should do.

And if I stay, I vow to be the best classroom pet I can possibly be, cross my toes!

Of course, if I have to go to Piney Woods, I will still Float. Doze. *Be.* But in Room 26, I've learned that there's a lot more to life than sitting on a lily pad.

I've learned that a little critter can make a big difference to humans. Humphrey has done that, and I want to do it, too.

The room is very quiet as Mr. Morales reaches into the box and reads the first vote.

"Piney Woods," he says.

My heart sinks down to the tips of my webbed toes.

But the next vote is "Room Twenty-six."

And then there's another.

My mind races as he reads the votes off one by one.

In the end, there are two votes for Piney Woods. The rest are all for me to stay in Room 26.

"I guess that's a clear choice," Mr. Morales says. "Og will remain as your classroom pet."

There are cheers and cheers and more cheers!

I am cheering, too! Even Heidi and Garth join in.

I hear some very lively squeaking as well. Thank you, Humphrey!

Despite all the cheering, Mrs. Brisbane has a worried look on her face.

"But I'm concerned because I think there were more votes than there are students," she says.

Mr. Morales does a quick recount, and Mrs. Brisbane is right. "We have an extra vote. I *think* it might be this one."

He holds up a thin strip of paper that is much smaller than the others.

"The writing is so small, I can hardly read it," she says. "But it does say Room Twenty-six."

That's a relief, because if Humphrey didn't want me to stay, our lives as neighbors might be difficult.

She looks around the classroom. "Whose vote is this?"

No one raises a hand or answers.

"If someone tried to vote twice, I'd like to know about it," she says, studying the big tads' faces for a sign.

They all look so innocent. Because they *are* innocent.

And Humphrey doesn't squeak up because he didn't vote twice.

Mrs. Brisbane sighs. "I hope whoever this paper belongs to will let me know privately. Meanwhile, even without this vote, Og will stay."

The cheers are deafening!

BING-BANG-BOING! My heart is hopping around. This is what I wanted all along. I just didn't know it.

Even with all the noise, I can hear a small, shrill voice.

"SQUEAK-SQUEAK-SQUEAK-SQUEAK-SQUEAK!"

"Thank you, Humphrey," I tell him. "Your vote counts with me!"

I think that we'll be going back to the normal routine in Room 26, but I am wrong.

A few days after the vote, Mrs. Brisbane makes an announcement. "Dr. Okeke has invited us to participate in this spring's Wildlife Fair at Piney Woods. But we have a lot of work to do to get ready."

"But you said it's not until spring," Garth says.

"Yes," Mrs. Brisbane replies. "And the first day of spring is just a little over a month away."

And what a month it is!

In addition to their usual lessons, my friends make big posters for our display at the fair.

Garth spends a lot of time recording me and I am hoppy to sing all of my favorite songs. But when he mixes them up on the tape, they don't sound quite as good as they do in the swamp.

Heidi and Gail make up a dance called the Frog Hop and teach it to all the big tads.

It's fun to watch Tabitha hop alongside Sayeh and Seth. Tabitha's giggling even louder than Gail!

"That will attract people to our display," Heidi explains.

"I hope it doesn't drive them away," Richie mutters.

Mrs. Brisbane likes the dance. "But I think we also need to tell people why frogs are threatened and what they can do to help."

So my friends get busy making posters, and they show them to me.

A.J. makes a drawing of a beautiful pond—with people picking up the trash around it. It says KEEP OUR RIVERS AND STREAMS CLEAN across the top.

Garth draws some bottles with scary labels and puts X's through them. He writes: KEEP CHEMICALS OUT OF OUR WATER.

Mandy's poster has a big factory pumping out black smoke with DON'T POLLUTE in huge letters.

And Sayeh's looks just like McKenzie's Marsh with drawings of all the animals who live there. It says PROTECT OUR MARSHES!

"Thank you, friends!" I tell them.

Hearing about all those problems makes me glad I live in a nice clean tank in Room 26!

"We can take Og to the fair, can't we?" Tabitha asks one day.

Mrs. Brisbane thinks that's a wonderful idea—and so do I!

"But what about Humphrey?" A.J. asks. "He's wildlife, too."

Gail giggles. "I never saw a hamster in the woods."

A.J. shrugs. "Maybe not, but hamsters must live in the wild somewhere."

Mrs. Brisbane says he has a point. "I'll call Dr. Okeke and see if we can take both of them."

And that's how Humphrey and I end up at the Piney Woods Wildlife Fair a few weeks later.

There's plenty of wildlife there, from eagles (I just can't look at those sharp beaks) to somebody walking around in a bear suit. It doesn't look like any bear I've ever seen.

The *wildest* wildlife of all are the humans.

The Frog Hop does attract a lot of people to the display table, where folks of all ages show up to admire Humphrey and me. And that gives the big tads a chance to talk about how frogs are disappearing.

That's terrible news, but the kids are excited to tell people how they can take action and help protect the frogs that are left. And all the other animals, too.

I even know some of the humans who arrive. There are some parents, of course. Aldo comes, too, with his nice wife, Maria. She tells me I'm the cutest frog she's ever seen.

I think I'm making quite a splash!

And I'm thrilled when the principal, Mr. Morales, stops by with his children.

"Og is a very important addition to Longfellow School," he tells them. "Just like Humphrey."

Now, that makes me want to jump for joy!

All in all, Piney Woods is a pretty nice place. I probably would like it there.

I wouldn't have to spend my days on the lookout for enemies, like Chopper, and searching for food. But I wouldn't have my swamp friends to play with.

I also wouldn't have big tads to look after. I wouldn't have real problems to solve.

I wouldn't have a *job*. And I wouldn't have a friend named Humphrey.

I'm so glad it's settled. I'm the second classroom pet of Room 26. The first classroom pet is a tough act to follow, but I'll give it a try.

I still think of my friends in the swamp, of course. But it's just like that song Mrs. Brisbane sang. I've made new silver friends, but I haven't forgotten the old ones, the gold ones.

I even wrote a poem about it, just like my friends did for the poetry festival.

To my friends in the swamp far away,
I wish you could hear what I say.
From our first days as tads,
On those green lily pads,
You are very special to me.

We had good days and bad days to weather,
And we always did it together.
You were friends good and true,
And I'm telling you,
You are very special to me.

We had a ball,
But time changes all,
And I didn't know
That I'd have to go.
We're apart, but I still think of you.
There are new things that I've got to do.

But the memories stay,
And to this very day . . .
You are very special to me—
You'll always be special to me.

It's a good poem, I think. And now it's time to Float.
Doze. *Be.*

Sing-Along Suggestions
🐾 🐾 for Og's Songs 🐾 🐾

All of Og's songs can be sung to familiar melodies. Have fun singing!

Keep reading for a sneak peek into Og's next adventure!

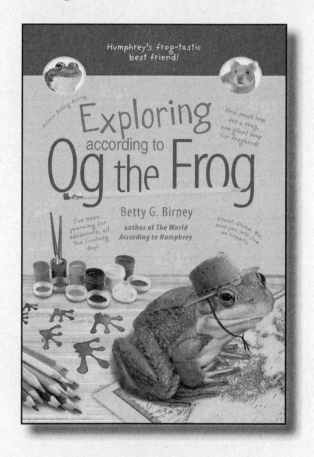

Boxed In

· · · · · · · · · · · · · · · · · ·

There's so much to see in the swamp: blue sky, mucky brown water, green lily pads, and all kinds of colorful (and yummy) insects. As our teacher, Granny Greenleaf, told us little tads in the swamp, "If you want a view, the swamp is for you!" Why would anyone ever want to leave? And even if someone did, how would he begin? As a young tad, I had no idea.

In Room 26, the view is very different from the swamp!

I have only lived at Longfellow School for a short time, but luckily, I'm a clever frog, and I caught on to life in the classroom in a hurry. Right now, though, I am looking at something strange even for a classroom—a sea of boxes.

Boxes are everywhere!

One thing I've learned is that although frogs and other swamp creatures like me love living out in the open near

1

water, humans prefer to live in boxes. Their houses may all look different, but to my froggy eyes, they are all boxes, divided into smaller boxes called rooms.

Not only do humans live in boxes, so do hamsters!

At least Humphrey does, and he's the only hamster I know. He lives in a box with sides made of bars, called a cage. It sits on a table by the window, right next to my tank.

I, at least, have glass walls and some water, but it's still a lot different from the way I lived back in the swamp not so long ago.

And now our teacher, Mrs. Brisbane, has the class building a little town with houses and buildings made from—you guessed it—boxes.

As we say in the swamp, "Whatever makes you hoppy!"

"SQUEAK-SQUEAK-SQUEAK!" my neighbor shouts.

Humphrey's squeaks sound cheerful, maybe because they've named the little town Humphreyville. I'm never sure what he's thinking, though, because I haven't understood a word he's said so far! And he clearly doesn't understand my green frog "BOINGs."

The humans don't, either. They don't understand that "BOING-BOING" might mean "thank you." Or "BOING-BOING" might mean "good job!" They think one boing is like another, which isn't true.

At least I've been able to figure out what humans are saying.

"Don't forget the small details of your house," Mrs. Brisbane reminds the big tads. "And think about the other town buildings as well, like the school and city hall."

More boxes.

Mandy Payne works on the biggest box of all. "I'm making a huge, fancy house with lots of windows," she says. "And my own room."

"What kind of dinosaur can jump higher than a house?" Kirk asks.

"You tell us," Mrs. Brisbane says. She knows Kirk likes to tell jokes.

"All of them!" he answers. "Houses can't jump."

BING-BANG-BOING! How does he think of these things?

The class settles down, and I look around the room. As usual, everything is bright and clean. (Especially after a man named Aldo comes in with his broom and mop each weeknight.)

It's nothing like the swamp, which is a wonderland of mud, pond scum and damp grass.

I don't think most humans would like to live in the swamp, but many other creatures do. Not just frogs, but slithery snakes, lizards and turtles, cranes and eagles, bats, owls, and tasty treats like dragonflies, mosquitoes and—yum—crickets.

We frogs like a home that's a bit damp and mucky. I

don't even mind some glorious goo. As our teacher, Granny Greenleaf, taught us, "A place that's wetter is a place that's better. Get too dry, and it's *bye-bye!*"

I think about the mud, and after a while, I hear a melody in my head. Before I even know it, I've thought up a song.

I like writing poems and songs in my spare time. I get an idea and let it splash around in my brain, and suddenly, I'm singing. This time, my song is about my ideal home.

How I love a mucky home,
Mucky home,
Mucky home!
How I love a mucky home,
One with a water view.

I love a house that drips a bit,
Drips a bit,
Drips a bit!
I love a house that drips a bit,
With gunk and grime and goo.

I love a home with bugs nearby,
Bugs nearby,
Bugs nearby!
I love a home with bugs nearby
If I can grab a few!

Don't get the wrong idea. My tank isn't bad. It's half land and half water, so I can take a dip anytime I feel a little dry. Mrs. Brisbane's husband, Bert, has added a lot of greenery, and I get good treats (though not as many juicy, wiggly crickets as I'd like).

The bell rings for recess, and it's time for me to relax in the water and let my mind roam free.

Float. Doze. *Be.*

Today, my mind roams back to McKenzie's Marsh, where I used to live before I was frognapped and brought here to Longfellow School. My name was Bongo then, but the students in Miss Loomis's class didn't know that, so they called me Og. I don't mind.

I was scared when the man took me from the swamp, but I don't think he knew he was doing a bad thing. In fact, he looked at me and said, "You are a good-looking frog. A real prince of a frog!" A prince—really? Did he know something I don't know?

Then he gave me to his grandson, who brought me to school to be a classroom pet.

Life wasn't all lily pads and lah-de-dah there in the swamp. I was always trying to catch enough food to fill my belly . . . without ending up as dinner for a bigger creature! Here in Room 26, I have no enemies, at least so far. I don't have to hunt because humans throw food into my tank.

But sometimes I get a tiny bit *bored.* I keep busy

swimming, hopping and watching my furry neighbor. Of course, I also write songs and poems.

My memories of the swamp fade away when the students—I think of them as big tadpoles—return from recess. Mrs. Brisbane tells them to get out their math books, and the door opens.

"Welcome, Paul," Mrs. Brisbane says. "Please come right in."

Hey, I know that boy! It's Paul Fletcher.

"Class, some of you may know Paul Fletcher from Miss Loomis's class. He is going to be coming into our class for math," our teacher says.

"Hi, friend!" I boing. He is usually in Room 27, where I lived for a little while. I liked it there, but a bullfrog named George was there first, and he badmouthed me from morning until night.

"**RUM-RUM. RUM-RUM!**" he'd repeat over and over.

He was as bad as Louie the Loudmouth, the leader of the bullying bullfrogs back in the swamp. Miss Loomis had to shout her lessons to be heard over George.

Paul passes by my tank on his way to his chair.

"Hi, Og," he says softly. "Glad to see you."

"BOING!" I answer softly. "Same here."

Some of the big tads make whispery noises, and Heidi points out that Paul is a year younger than the students in our class. That makes Paul stare down at the floor.

Mrs. Brisbane explains that even though he's a little bit younger, he is an excellent math student, so he will be studying with them.

And she's right. Even with George rum-rumming in Room 27, I could see Paul was good with numbers.

I don't know a lot about classroom math. In the swamp, all I needed to know about numbers is that one bullfrog is one bullfrog too many, and the best way to measure things is a hop, skip and a jump! But humans like to solve more difficult problems.

Mrs. Brisbane gives her students a tricky one that day. I even hear Art moan. The big tads work hard, but I can see that he and Mandy and a few other big tads are having trouble solving it by the way they chew their pencils and frown.

Paul has an easier time and finishes quickly.

"Way to go!" I shout, making a big splash when he puts his pencil down.

When math is over and Paul leaves, Heidi whispers to Gail, "What is he, some kind of brainiac?"

"More like a know-it-all," Gail mutters.

Kirk nods. "A real show-off."

A know-it-all and a show-off? I'd say Paul is on the ball and a smart student.

Mrs. Brisbane overhears them and shakes her head. "There'll be none of that talk here," she says firmly. "Everyone in this classroom is good at something. For Paul, it's math. So no more name calling. *Ever.*"

The room gets quiet and stays that way.

The next day, Paul returns for math.

Mrs. Brisbane is writing on the board, and she doesn't hear Mandy whisper, "Here comes Mr. Know-It-All."

"Watch it!" I warn her. "BOING-BOING!"

Paul keeps his head down, listens to the teacher and solves the problems.

I remember something Granny Greenleaf once said back in the swamp. "Hold your head high, even when you're feeling low."

I've tried it, and it works. Sometimes, when you're feeling low down, it's hard to keep your chin up, but it makes you feel better. Stronger. Hoppier.

"Hold your head high!" I tell Paul.

Unfortunately, the big tads laugh. They're laughing at my boings, but I can see that Paul thinks they're laughing at him. Now I've made things worse when I was trying to make them better!

I feel as useless as a dragonfly with waterlogged wings.

Then Humphrey speaks up, too. "SQUEAK-SQUEAK-SQUEAK-SQUEAK-*SQUEAK*!"

The tads laugh again, and Paul's face gets redder.

"Class, stop laughing right now! We're here to learn,

and you're upsetting Humphrey and Og," Mrs. Brisbane says.

For once I understand what Humphrey is thinking. He doesn't like the big tads' rudeness, and neither do I. BING-BANG-*BOING*! I think we're making progress.

❧ ❧ ❧ ❧

Throughout the week, the big tads are as busy as beavers working on Humphreyville, which grows a little bit every day.

More boxes are added to the town along with a patch of green labeled OG THE FROG NATURE PRESERVE. I'm glad they didn't name a box after me!

When Paul comes in, some of the students roll their eyes. But at least they keep quiet, while Paul keeps his head down (which is the opposite of holding your head high).

Then comes Friday, the day when Mrs. Brisbane announces which student will take Humphrey home for the weekend.

Everybody always wants to take Humphrey home for the weekend.

I stay back in Room 26. Mrs. Brisbane says it's more difficult to take me home because my tank is so heavy. And I don't need to have food and water as often as Humphrey. For a small creature who is mostly fur, he sure eats a lot! And what he doesn't eat, he saves in his cheek pouch.

If you think eating crickets like I do is icky, imagine storing food in your cheeks! Eww!

Mandy is not so pleased when Mrs. Brisbane doesn't pick her to take Humphrey home. "I never get to take him," she complains. Mrs. Brisbane points out that she has not returned a signed permission slip from her parents, which makes Mandy as flustered as a snapping turtle with weak jaws.

Seth lets out a whoop when he learns that he will have Humphrey for the weekend. He is a friendly human, but he has a hard time sitting still. He taps and twitches. He jiggles and wiggles. Sometimes, I get tired just watching him!

I think Humphrey will have his paws full at Seth's house this weekend, while I will have plenty of time to think.

Maybe I'll figure out what I can do to help Paul feel comfortable in our class.

After Aldo leaves Friday night (thanks to him for giving me some extra food), I have the classroom all to myself, and now I have a clear view of the houses in Humphreyville. They're all different, but every one is made from a box.

My fellow swamp creatures live in many kinds of homes. There are nests for the birds, while bats like a comfy crack in a tree. Beavers think big, building huge lodges out of wood.

Other creatures—like me and my frog friends—find our shelter under logs and leaves wherever we roam. That's right, I am a roaming kind of creature. Or at least I was before I became a classroom pet and got boxed in.

But here in my nice clean tank, at least I have some water, rocks and a bit of muck.

How many times did Granny Greenleaf tell us, "Whatever you do, wherever you are, make the most of your time, and you'll go far!"?

I get busy on my exercise routine so that even if I'm stuck in a tank, I'll still be the great leaper I was back in the swamp. First, I splash. I mean, I really *splash*.

Next come my jumping jacks. With each leap, I try to go a little higher. While I do, I think of my best frog friend in the swamp, Jumpin' Jack. We were both high jumpers, *and* I could understand everything he said, unlike my new friend Humphrey!

Push-ups are next on my list, followed by a series of giant leaps across my rock.

To finish, I swim so many laps, I lose count. Maybe I should pay more attention in math class, the way Paul does.

By the time I finish, it's already starting to get dark outside. After all, it's winter.

I relax on my rock and take some deep breaths. Time to Float. Doze. *Be.*

I am so relaxed after all that exercise that I fall fast asleep.

When I wake up, it's morning. Right away, I realize something is strange. The light is different than on other days. I turn to look toward the window, and I see it: snow.

I sit and stare for a long time because it's so white and so beautiful.

If I were still in the swamp, I'd be taking a long winter's nap. It's called hibernating.

I guess Jumpin' Jack and all my green frog pals in the swamp are hibernating now. They're not watching the fluffy snowflakes silently paint the world white. Think of all they're missing!

As I stare out at the white world, a little song starts forming in my brain.

It's a quiet song, like a lullaby, and I imagine I'm singing it to my friends.

Rock-a-bye, frog friends,
Down in the ice,
I hope the dreams
You're dreaming are nice.

When you awaken,
Down in the deep,
Think about all
You missed while asleep!

The song seems sad, but surprisingly, I feel a whole lot better! (Singing can do that for you. Try it!)

It wasn't my choice to move from the swamp to the classroom, but I suddenly see it as a great opportunity that few frogs ever have.

Unlike my friends sleeping in the swamp, I'm fully awake to see winter. I have dozens of new friends of strange but interesting species. Not only humans, but a *hamster*! Up until now, I thought Granny Greenleaf and wise old Uncle Chinwag knew everything, but believe me, they've never even heard of a hamster.

I have seen some amazing things back in the swamp. I once saw a water moccasin tie himself in a knot. And I saw a bullfrog with hiccups leap across six lily pads *and* the back of a snapping turtle, and he lived to tell about it.

But now a door has opened to the world of humans (and hamsters), and I, an adventurous, roaming green frog, would like to explore it. I want to go where no green frog has dared to go before.

I'll make a big splash! I may even become a legend like Sir Hiram Hopwell, the most famous frog ever.

Tomorrow, when the big tads and Mrs. Brisbane return to Room 26, I will be all ears (even though you can't see them) and all eyes (which are large and alert) so I can learn more than any frog ever has about all kinds of humans and the human world.

On Monday morning, I feel like a different frog. I'm rested, in great shape and ready to begin my mission.

When Seth brings Humphrey back to our shelf by the window, he says, "Thanks, Humphrey. I had the best weekend *ever!*"

Later I notice something new. Seth starts to fidget, but Humphrey squeaks, and Seth settles down. Then it happens again.

I'm puzzling over that when the door opens and the principal of Longfellow School, Mr. Morales, walks in. Whenever he enters, my classmates snap to attention. Even Humphrey rushes up his tree branch for a better look.

And Mr. Morales always wears the most interesting ties! Once he even wore one with funny frogs on it.

He tells Mrs. Brisbane that he's stopped in to see how Humphreyville is coming along.

"SQUEAK-SQUEAK-SQUEAK!" my neighbor says.

"Seems like a great place to live," Mr. Morales says after looking around. "Good work."

After he leaves, our teacher assigns the big tads jobs in the classroom. I don't understand most of them, like "line monitor" or "pencil patrol." There are no familiar jobs like "cricket catcher" or "helpful hopper." But when Miranda is given the job of "animal keeper," I know that she'll be looking after Humphrey and me.

That's a good thing, because Miranda is as responsible as Cousin Lucy Lou, who never showed up late for Granny

Greenleaf's class and never missed a leaping practice. She wasn't a high hopper, but she tried harder than any of us.

Good old Lucy Lou. I wonder if she misses me.

When the bell rings at the end of the day, Miranda comes over to my tank and bends down so we are eye to eye.

"Og, I'm going to take really good care of you!" she says. "Because I got the best job!"

"Thanks, Miranda," I answer, with a big boing!

She turns to Humphrey, who is peering out from his cage. "You too, Humphrey! I promise I'll be the greatest animal keeper ever!"

He answers with an encouraging "Squeak!"

Before she heads for the door, I see her check his cage door to make sure it's locked.

She is already a first-class animal keeper!

"Good job!" I tell her.

But I guess all she hears is "BOING!"

My Mission Begins

· · · · · · · · · · · · · · · · ·

*I*t's good to think outside of the swamp once in a while," Granny Greenleaf told the other young tads and me. "Like Sir Hiram Hopwell, the famed frog explorer." We all dreamed of being as adventurous as Sir Hiram. "He was as brave as they come, but he wasn't foolish," Granny explained. "He planned his expeditions carefully to make sure he didn't run into trouble. So use your heads, little tads, and try not to get into trouble in the first place!"

It's morning, and already there's big trouble in Room 26. And I mean BIG!

Humphrey is trapped in his cage . . . and I can't do a thing to help him! He looks as miserable as if he were in jail. And I bet he feels like he's in jail, too!

The furry guy has a secret way of opening the lock on his cage and getting out. I've seen him do it with my own big froggy eyes. Somehow, he always manages to get back in his cage before humans see him.

Until last night. He opened the lock and scurried over to squeak at me. He was pretty upset about something. I tried to warn him that it was time for Aldo to arrive to clean, but he waited a few seconds too long. Aldo found him on the table!

After he put Humphrey back in his cage, Aldo took a paper clip and bent it around the door so it couldn't swing open.

Poor Humphrey spent the whole night trying to unbend the paper clip with his paws and teeth, but it didn't work.

Worse yet, Aldo left a note for Mrs. Brisbane telling her all about what happened.

And now, in front of the whole class, Mrs. Brisbane is blaming Miranda for leaving Humphrey's cage door unlocked.

"BOING-BOING! BOING-BOING!" I try to tell her she's wrong.

Humphrey does too. "SQUEAK-SQUEAK-SQUEAK!"

Of course, nobody can understand us.

"But I *did* lock the cage," Miranda tells the teacher. "I remember."

I remember, too, but Mrs. Brisbane doesn't believe her!

She is very serious as she says that Miranda didn't do her job . . . and she tells her to switch jobs with Art.

I guess everybody makes a mistake now and then, but this time it isn't Miranda who is in the wrong. It's our teacher! When Miranda begins to cry, I feel as helpless as a turtle stuck in its shell. Only, I am a frog stuck in a glass box, and I don't even have a door to jiggle open.

My mood improves a little bit when Mrs. Brisbane takes the paper clip off my neighbor's cage to check the lock. She sees that it's not broken—but Humphrey and I already knew that.

Despite her tears, Miranda manages to pull herself together and apologize to Mrs. Brisbane.

That was brave of her! It's not easy to say you're sorry when you did your best. But being brave means doing the right thing even if it's uncomfortable. I wonder if I could do what Miranda did.

One thing I've discovered about humans: They all make mistakes at one time or another. They're lucky, because if my friends in the swamp make a mistake, it usually means they meet an unfortunate end.

Mrs. Brisbane may not end up as a snapping turtle's supper, but she sure made a big mistake.

I'm hoppy that as the week continues, nobody mentions the cage door in class. Every afternoon, Mrs. Brisbane's students have been sharing their book reports, and today, it's A.J.'s turn.

"My book isn't a made-up story," he says. "Mine is all true."

"That's fine." Mrs. Brisbane nods. "That's called nonfiction."

"It's about as nonfiction as they come," A.J. says. "It's called *Tales of the Great Explorers*, and it tells the stories of real people who made great discoveries—lots of them."

I don't know anything about nonfiction or what that means, but I am interested in making discoveries. I wonder if there are any frog explorers in the book.

"Some of them traveled a long way over the sea, like Magellan and Balboa," he says. "And some traveled a long way over land, like Marco Polo and a guy named Louis Clark."

"They were two men," Mrs. Brisbane corrects him. "Lewis *and* Clark."

"That's them," A.J. says. "They explored all the western part of the United States when it was really wild."

I find this story *very* interesting. Almost as interesting as the stories Uncle Chinwag told about the famous frog adventurer, Sir Hiram Hopwell.

"Then there were explorers who went to outer space. They were astronauts who were launched in spaceships. Neil Armstrong was the first person ever to set foot on the moon." A.J. holds the book up to show a picture of a person on the moon.

This gets my blood pumping, because sometimes, when I start out with a huge leap, I feel as if *I'm* being launched into space.

"He said, 'One small step for man, one giant leap for mankind,'" A.J. continues.

He sure is a great leaper. Maybe Neil Armstrong was part frog!

"And did you come away from reading the book with some new ideas?" Mrs. Brisbane asks.

A.J. thinks for a moment. "At the end, the author says there are still places to explore and discover. I think that would be a cool job!"

Mrs. Brisbane chuckles. "Yes, indeed—if you like a challenge."

Heidi waves her hand wildly until the teacher calls on her.

"Aren't there any girl explorers?" She wrinkles her nose. "Were there only boys in the book?"

A.J. assures her there were girls. "Sure! There are women astronauts. And this one lady, she was the one who led that Louis Clark guy on his journey because she already knew where she was going."

"Then why can't we read about her?" Heidi wants to know. I think it's a good question.

"You can," Mrs. Brisbane says. "There are many good books in the library about female astronauts like Sally Ride, as well as Sacagawea, the Native American woman who guided Lewis and Clark. And you can look up some other explorers, like Amelia Earhart."

She glances at the clock. "Looks like it's time to announce who is taking Humphrey home this weekend," she says.

The room gets so quiet, you could hear a mosquito burp.

When Art is chosen, he looks as pleased as a green frog (me!) with a nice, fresh cricket!

Once Humphrey is gone and the classroom is empty, it's time for me to get hop-hopping.

A.J.'s report about explorers has made me even more excited about my new mission to explore the human world. But to succeed, I'm going to have to figure out a way to get out of my tank.

Oh, yes, I can pop the top off. I've already done that a couple of times.

The problem is this: What happens once I'm out of the tank?

I need to focus, so I decide to take some time to Float. Doze. *Be.*

The gentle movement of the water helps me think, and I realize there are three problems. First, if I do leave the tank, I will start to dry out after a while. Not right away, but it's always wise to stay a little damp.

Also, I can pop the top of my tank and get out onto the table, but how do I get back *into* my tank? It's not as simple as walking through a cage door.

Finally, even if I figure out solutions to the first two problems, how do I safely get off the tabletop and into the broader world . . . and back again?

All this thinking has made me tired, but it takes a long time to fall asleep in the dark silence. In the swamp, night is my most awake time. I miss the sounds of owl hoots, bat wings flapping, singing crickets and the occasional scream of a red fox in the woods. (Well, maybe I don't miss that last one.)

I drift off, and when I wake up, sunbeams are dancing across the table. I take that to be a good sign.

It's the perfect day to start my new quest to explore the human world!

I do some warm-up leaps, preparing for the big moment when I pop the top of my tank. My goal is to move it just enough to make room to get out without knocking the top completely off. I work out how many jumps it will take.

Then I go for a quick dip, to make sure I'm as damp as I can be.

Ten, nine, eight, seven, six, five, four, three, two, one, and I have liftoff! If only Jumpin' Jack could see me!

After a nice, soft landing on the sack of Humphrey's

favorite snack, Nutri-Nibbles, I slide down and hop over to the edge of the table. I look down.

It's a lot farther than a hop, skip and a jump, believe me. Humphrey slides down the table leg to get to the floor. Then he swings his way back up using the blinds' cord.

I could probably manage both the table leg and the swinging if I happened to be a tree frog, which I am not. (Don't even get me started on those guys. Tiny frogs with their heads in the clouds. I prefer my feet near the ground, thank you!)

Tree frogs' toes are as sticky as glue, but my toes are only a little sticky, so I couldn't walk down the table leg like them. If I tried sliding the way Humphrey does, I'd probably have a very bumpy ride. Or tumble right off and land on my head.

Next, I examine the blinds' cord.

It's long and is made up of two slender ropes. Near the bottom, they are tied together, forming a little U shape.

I stare hard at that cord, trying to figure out if I can do anything with it. Humphrey uses it to get back up to our table. He grabs the cord with both paws, wraps his tiny toes around it and swings back and forth. Each time it goes a little higher.

Then—BING-BANG-BOING!—he lets go of the cord and leaps onto the tabletop!

It's incredibly brave of him.

Or incredibly dumb. Sometimes it's hard to tell the difference between brave and dumb.

I'm sure Louie the Loudmouth thought he was being brave and smart when he rum-rummed loudly at a passing group of ducks to ruffle their feathers. But because he wasn't paying attention, a long-legged crane swooped down and carried Louie away.

I'll bet the ducks quacked up about that!

I'm trying not to do anything too brave or too dumb, but something just right.

If I can't grasp the table leg, I can't grasp the cord, either.

I stare at that little U-shaped spot some more. It reminds me of a chair. Frogs don't sit in chairs, of course, but I think I could fit in it. But how would I get there in the first place?

I look down over the edge of the table again.

I don't think I'm brave enough to try it. Or maybe I'm not dumb enough. Either way, I'm going to have to think about how to get down there very carefully.

I climb up the bag of Nutri-Nibbles and dive back into my tank. At least the glass box is safe, and the water feels good on my skin as I splash around.

As I drift in the water, I think of a new verse for my song.

Rock-a-bye gently,
All through the night.
Have I solved the problem?
I must say not quite.

When I awaken
And morning is here,
I hope that the answer
Will become clear!

In the morning, I stare at the top of my tank. It is still open from my escape yesterday.

If I do manage to conquer the problem of the cord, I don't want my teacher and classmates to realize that I'm escaping my glass box.

But how in the swamp can I put the top back into position?

It's a good thing I'm an exceptional leaper: For most of the morning, I leap up and tap the top again and again. Each time, it moves a tiny bit.

Using the trial-and-error method, I tap it here, tap it there, until eventually it settles back into place.

It's still a little crooked, but maybe no one will notice.

I think Granny Greenleaf would be pleased, too. After all, she's the one who taught me, "If at first you don't succeed, leap, leap again."

I still have time for a nice doze, so I'm all rested up when Humphrey and the rest of my friends in Room 26 return from the weekend.

My furry neighbor seems excited to see me. I wish I could understand what he's squeaking about, but Art seems happy, so I think he and Humphrey had a good weekend.

When Paul comes in the room for math class, I notice a big change.

Usually, Paul hurries to his seat and never says a word—not even to me!

But today, he seems more relaxed. When he passes by Art's desk, they bump fists and Paul whispers something in Art's ear.

And they describe how Humphrey took an exciting train ride. I thought he went to Art's house. Did Paul end up there, too? And *what* train ride? Where did the little guy go?

All I can tell is that a big change took place over the weekend—Art and Paul are now friends. And Humphrey had something to do with it.

No time to think about that now because Mrs. Brisbane announces a pop math quiz. I didn't see this one coming. I hope the big tads don't pop *their* tops!

Paul quickly whizzes through the answers, while Art just stares at the paper. When he finally picks up his pencil, I can tell he's having a rough time, but he finishes the quiz.

It takes Mrs. Brisbane all the lunch period and then some to mark the tests. Humphrey stares at her and nibbles his toes. He's as nervous as a mouse passing by the spooky owl tree at midnight. And there's nothing more dangerous than *that*!

I slip into the water and drift until I hear Mrs. Brisbane announce that she is finished.

I can see by Art's smiling face that he did better than he expected.

Mandy got an F. An F should be a good thing! It could even stand for *Frog*. But the F makes Mandy look as unhappy as a long-necked crane with a sore throat.

"I can't believe I failed," she mumbles.

So that's it. F is for *Failed*.

Mrs. Brisbane tells her she can take the test again. If she passes *and* if she brings in a paper signed by her parents, she can take Humphrey home for the weekend.

Everybody always wants to take Humphrey home for the weekend, but so far, Mrs. Brisbane is the only human who has taken me home.

I wonder if *that* will ever change.

Read about Og's exciting time
at summer camp in

Wildlife
according to
Og the Frog

coming soon!

More books about adventures in Room 26 by Betty G. Birney